Virtual Imaginings

INKBLOT BOOKS
VACAVILLE, CA

Virtual Imaginings

Published by Inkblot Books
www.inkblotbooks.com

Cover image ©2009 C.S. Marks
www.elfhunter.net

ISBN-10: 1932461221
ISBN-13: 9781932461220

Printed in the United States of America

Virtual

Imaginings

~Broken~
R.J. Keller
-1-

~The Accordian~
J. Dean
-4-

~Coping with Breast Cancer~
Ricky Sides
-15-

~The Last Step~
Michael E. Thompson
-35-

~Cat Feathers~
Brendan Carroll
-47-

~Pound of Flesh~
Richard Gerard
-54-

~Purgatory~
Maria Rachel Hooley
-68-

~Being Regular~
K.A. Thompson
-84-

~America, Land of Mystery~
Ricky Sides
-94-

~Dime a Dip~
Edward Cliffe Patterson
-106-

~Uncle Aleister~
Randolph Lalonde
-119-

~Angel of Death~
Richard Gerard
-128-

~The Frogs of Orange Tree~
Christopher L. Hughes
-130-

~The Land of Fear~
William Woodall
-149-

~Sam~
K.A. Thompson
-172-

A special thanks to Megan Cullor for proof reading each story and finding all our mistakes.

Broken

R.J. Keller

He wasn't surprised to hear the knock on his door, even though it was nearly midnight. He'd been expecting it for almost a month, half hoping each night that she'd work up the nerve so they could just get it over with.

She looked almost regal, standing there on his battered porch, dripping with wealth. She'd even had the audacity to wear her gaudy diamond wedding ring. He wasn't irritated by it, though. It seemed fitting. She'd come here to proposition him, but she still needed to keep him in his place.

Finally she spoke. "I understand you're finished with remodeling our kitchen."

He nodded.

"I suppose that means we won't be seeing you at the house again anytime soon."

He nodded again, not giving her so much

as a smile. If she wanted him, she'd have to come out with it. So she pressed on, annoyed, but too desperate to walk away.

"I...heard your girlfriend left you."

It was actually the other way around, but he didn't correct her. It didn't matter. The result was the same. He was still left with nothing but a bruised ego, an empty heart, and something to prove.

And this rich, beautiful woman had knocked on his door, begging him to prove it.

But he'd been with this kind of woman before. She'd wasted her youth on a man who would toss her aside when Youth was gone. She knew it. And now she was empty, just like him. She practically reeked of it.

I need. I want. Give me.

Because she had nothing left to give.

Neither did he. So he closed the door without a word. Because he wasn't that broken. Not yet.

R.J. Keller is a writer from Central Maine, where she lives happily with her husband, two kids, and the family cat. In addition to writing angsty novels, Kel enjoys gardening, rooting for the Boston Red Sox, and watching other people cook. She is also an avid movie buff, able to recite every line from "The Princess Bride," "Gettysburg," and "Bull Durham" with her eyes closed.

She is the author of *Waiting For Spring*, a novel that takes readers beyond the lighthouses and rocky beaches tourists visit and drops them instead into a rural Maine town that is filled with displaced factory workers who struggle with poverty and loss, yet push onward with stubbornness and humor.

The Accordion
J. Dean

The initial shouting phase had ended. By now, the "discussion" as they called it, although still carrying heated undercurrents, had at least settled to a somewhat civil tone, which made Sandra feel a little bit less knotted inside, although the nausea did not entirely leave her stomach. Seated on her bed with crossed legs, she looked around her room, pink and pony-decorated, trying to draw from familiar comfort that was absorbed from the toys and dolls that occupied her shelves and table. At best, it only gave a superficial sense of relief; she knew that eventually that relief would dissipate when her parents came in after finishing their "not-an-argument" argument about what to do with her.

Her fingers wormed their way around each other in her lap, restlessly fidgeting in anticipation. Equally unsettled was the rational side of her eight-year-old brain, debating with itself on how to answer once the questions started coming. In reality, there was only one real solution: tell the truth. Aside from the conviction ingrained into her heart that lying was wrong, no other explanation could be given that would satisfy either Mommy or Daddy. After all, they did walk in on her in the middle of the deed, and any other story, no matter how fantastically her imaginative side tried to conceive, just wouldn't pass.

Nope. No other way to do it. Just tell the truth, no matter what.

They won't believe her, of course. Adults never did, not when the circumstances cast any sort of reasonable doubt on the child. Sandra shook her head at that thought. What a terrible time adults have, not possessing the imagination to consider other alternatives to explain things that don't make sense. How on earth do they make it through life by looking at it through such boring and faithless eyes?

The discussion had ceased. In its place, two pairs of footfalls on the hall floor softly thumped toward her. She swung her jean-clad legs and bare feet over the edge of the bed, standing upright, brushing her pink shirt unconsciously to smooth out wrinkles that may or may not have been there.

Time to tell the truth.

**

They came in slowly, Mommy first, with her shoulder-length curly blond hair and pretty, round face. Behind and above her was the face of Daddy, square and perfect, with close-cropped hair and his thin-rimmed glasses.

How smart Daddy looks with those glasses, Sandra thought to herself.

"Honey," Daddy began, "before we talk, I want to apologize for yelling at you like that."

Sandra shrugged. "'sokay," she replied softly, looking at the floor.

"No, honey, it's not okay. I should have-Sandra, please look at me. Thank you-I should have asked what was going on before exploding like I did. No matter what you were doing, or why, I should have used more self-control. Please forgive me for that."

She nodded. "I do."

Daddy gave a weak smile and a nod. "Thank you, baby."

Mommy approached her and kneeled. She put a hand on Sandra's arm. "We love you, Sandra. But when we came home and saw you, we panicked. To tell the truth, you really caught us off guard, honey."

Sandra nodded slowly. *Here it comes*, she thought.

"So why exactly did you do that to Grandpa's accordion?" Daddy asked.

Sandra looked up at him. "If I tell you, will you promise not to yell?"

"I won't yell, honey."

"Promise?"

"Yes, I promise."

"Because the accordion was after me."

Both Mommy and Daddy wrinkled their faces in puzzled frustration. "What do you mean?" Mommy asked.

"You don't believe me."

"Whether we do or not, I still want to hear your side of things," Daddy replied honestly. Sandra looked at him, searching his face for any sort of mocking expression, but saw none.

"So how do you know the accordion was after you?" Mommy asked.

Sandra looked down again, taking a deep breath. "It started last week, Mommy. At bedtime. It came in my room and talked to me."

"And how did it do that?"

"It crawled, Mommy."

"What, you mean like with legs?" Daddy asked.

Sandra firmly shook her head. "No. Like-like those caterpillars on TV, Daddy, how they get short and then long again, and move that way. The accordion did that. It got short and long, in that middle part."

"You mean the bellows?"

Sandra nodded. "I heard it come in. And

it said my name each time it moved, with that weird music it plays. It spoke like that."

Mommy looked up at Daddy, who returned her look with an uncertain shrug. "I think I remember that night. Is that why you came to bed with us?"

Sandra bobbed her head down in affirmation. "And it tried to get me when I left, too. It was scary, Daddy. It had eyes, green glowing eyes. It was a monster. I was so scared, Daddy."

Her voice began to crack slightly. A tear dropped down her left cheek. Mommy took her up in a hug. Daddy stepped forward with a soft, smoothing touch on her blond hair. "Hey, hey. It's okay, sweetie."

"Are you sure it wasn't just a dream, Sandra? I came in your room the next day, and I didn't see the accordion."

Sandra sniffed hard. "No, Mommy. It was no dream." Another few sniffs accompanied a couple of sobs as she buried her head in Mommy's shoulder.

"Sandra, honey," Daddy asked, "Did it happen again?"

She looked up at him through moistened eyes. "Yes." A smile crossed her face, "but I chased it away."

"How did you do that?"

She pointed to the corner of her room, in which sat a small aluminum baseball bat. "It came in again, and it was saying

'Sandra... get you... Sandra.... get you' in that awful music voice. And I saw those green eyes at the door again. It was coming toward me. I screamed, Mommy. I screamed, but you didn't hear me."

Mommy and Daddy both shook their heads. "No, we don't remember that, baby."

"But it was okay." Sandra puffed her chest out a bit as Mommy set her down, her fear giving way to bravado. "I got out of bed and got the bat. It kept coming, and I hit it- wham! Right on its front, where those black and white buttons are!"

"The keys?"

"Yeah! You should have seen me, Daddy! I hit it, and it ran! It was afraid of me 'cause I hit it! It turned around and ran back!"

Mommy immediately looked back at Daddy again, a shocked look on her face. "What?" he asked her.

"I'll tell you later," she answered. "So, what happened after that?"

"Remember Sally coming over yesterday?" Sandra asked. Both parents did.

"Well, when she was over and we were having tea time, it tried to come in again! It peeked around the corner at us, and it was not happy at me. Oh, Daddy, it talked to me again, and said 'get you.. get you...' in the music voice, but the music voice was angry. Really angry!"

"And Sally saw it?"

"Yes she did! And I picked up my bat and started walking toward the accordion, but that chicken accordion just ran off. And Sally was scared, so I didn't go run off after it. I stayed with her. She ran home crying right after."

"I wondered why she didn't stay for dinner," Mommy mused.

"So," Daddy spoke, "when did you decide to get my hunting knife down from my dresser?"

She pressed her lips together. For a moment, she felt as if they actually were believing her. Now, Daddy's question seemed to change all of that. "Today," she answered quietly.

"Even though you knew that my hunting knife was off limits to you?" he asked, slightly more sternly.

Sandra nodded.

"I wish you'd keep that knife locked up somewhere else," Mommy murmured.

"There's never been a problem with it before," Daddy answered curtly, then looked at Sandra. "And what happened after that? Did the accordion come for you again?"

Sandra looked up at him. "But it came really fast, Daddy. So fast that it scared me. I had your knife, and waited on the bed, pretending to be taking a nap. And it came in again, saying 'Sandra... get you...' again in that creepy music voice! And when it came close to my bed, that's when I jumped down and started stabbing it!"

"Which is when we came in, right?" Mommy asked.

"That's right! But it's dead now, Grandpa's accordion is dead! It can't hurt me anymore, Daddy!"

Daddy let out a sigh, looking at Mommy. "Yeah... it's dead alright. Look, Sandra, I need to talk to Mommy again. You need to wait here for a little bit."

Sandra pouted her lip. "Are you two going to argue more?"

Mommy smiled and gave her a reassuring hug. "No, honey, we're not."

"No, we're not," Daddy added. "But this is a little weird, for us to come home and see our little girl stabbing the bellows of her grandpa's accordion."

"I know that," Sandra answered glumly. "I knew you'd think I was making it up. But you tell me to tell the truth, and I did."

They walked out, giving her each a set of hugs and kisses before leaving.

**

In the kitchen, the corpse of the victim awaited them, strewn out across the table, its bellows little more than punctured, slashed tatters of material, the black keyboard side of the instrument maliciously grinning at them, missing a few of its black and white teeth.

"What was the funny look for?" Daddy asked.

"Because I was in Sandra's room and found one of the broken keys on her floor, just under her bed," Mommy replied, pointing to one of the gaps where a white rectangle should be on the keyboard. "It was cracked in half."

"You think she really hit it with her bat?"

She gave him an exasperated expression. "Look what she did to it just a little bit ago, honey!"

"Yeah, yeah. Okay. So now what? We going to call a shrink or something?"

"We should call *somebody*, I think."

He shook his head. "But she's never done something like this before. Look, if she had been doing crazy things like this for a while, I can see calling somebody. But she's never given us a reason to think she's needed treatment like this."

Mommy let out a sigh through her nostrils, her eyes starting to brim with salty water. Daddy put his hand on her arm. "Just-Okay, look-go ahead and get the number of somebody. But let's give her a few days first, alright? I mean, it's not like she tried to stab one of us."

She looked up at him, smudging away tears. "And if she doesn't seem to be back to normal? Will you back me up if I call?"

"One hundred percent. I'll even lock my

hunting knife up in the gun cabinet too. Fair enough?"

Another hesitant exhalation of breath. "Alright."

He wrapped both arms around her. "She's fine, honey. Really. I'm sure of it."

Mommy nodded, a forced smile crossing her face. "Now get that thing off the table. I want to get dinner going."

Daddy chuckled. "Fine with me. I've been looking for an excuse to get rid of it."

"How did we end up with it anyway?"

Daddy was slowly pushing together the wrecked accordion, which replied with a feeble squeal of noise. "Funny enough," he said with a grunt, lifting the cumbersome mechanism up, "my brother Joey never liked that accordion. Dad would play his songs for us and Joey just didn't like it. Wouldn't touch it or walk near it. I never understood why."

He moved toward the door. Mommy moved to the kitchen radio, and cranked a dial. The radio responded with John Lennon telling her that he was the Walrus, goo-goo g'joob. Mommy rolled her eyes, adjusting the station to the more agreeable voice of Billy Joel loving her just the way she was.

A moment later, while in the middle of preparing the chicken, Daddy came back in, a strange look plastered on his face.

Mommy looked up. "What? What's

wrong?"

He turned his face toward her. "I'm hearing things."

"Why's that?"

"When I took the accordion out, and put it in the trash can, I could have sworn I heard it speak."

Mommy put her hands on her hips. "Don't tell me *you're* flipping out now!"

"No! I-I don't know, maybe I'm letting my imagination get the best of me. I put it in, and it expanded as I dropped it. You know, the bellows, did. But it made that typical accordion sound, and when it did, I could-alright, don't look at me like that! I know, I know-but it sure sounded like it, well, it *said* something!"

"And what did it say?"

Daddy pressed his lips together. "It said 'get you.'"

J. Dean is a writer and teacher from Michigan, the author of *The Summoning of Clade Josso: The First Descent into the Vein*, the first book of the Vein project, an epic series of "fantasy for those who don't normally read fantasy," available for Kindle. The preceding is a short story inspired by a humorous account given to him by one of his students, which prompted him to take the events and give them an eerie spin.

Coping With Breast Cancer

Ricky Sides

In the fall of 1995 we were living the good life. We'd just bought our dream house and moved in the previous July and were looking forward to our first holiday season in our new home. Only one thing placed a cloud over our lives at that point in time. My wife had a mysterious bloody discharge from one breast. She had also lost a considerable amount of weight and I was beginning to become concerned.

My wife was reluctant to agree to go to a doctor but finally I managed to elicit a promise from her that she would go to see a physician the day after Thanksgiving. That morning we got into our car for the drive to the doctor, never suspecting that our lives were about to be forever changed.

I sat in the waiting room while my wife saw her gynecologist. I saw her come back out just a few minutes after she had been escorted back to the examination room. She was pale and said that the doctor had told her we had to go to the hospital at once for a mammogram and that the doctor was calling ahead to get her worked in that day.

She broke down and cried on the drive to the hospital and expressed her sense of dread saying, "*The doctor says she's afraid it might be breast cancer.*" That was the first time I heard the words breast cancer in relation to my wife.

The doctor was true to her word and the people at the hospital were expecting my wife when we arrived. She was immediately hustled back into the radiology area where she underwent her first mammography at age 35.

Tensely I waited, not yet comprehending what was happening. My mind seemed numb, almost as if I had consumed a vast amount of alcohol. I guess I was in a sort of state of shock. I nervously thumbed through some brochures sitting in a rack in the waiting room. As I did so I told myself that there had to be some mistake. My wife couldn't have breast cancer. Not my Sue.

I didn't have long to wait. Soon my wife was back and she told me we now had to go to see another doctor in the city.

With an ever-growing sense of dread we headed to our car and drove to the next doctor's office where we scheduled an appointment to see the doctor the next day. We signed and filled out tons of paperwork in preparation for that visit and then left.

Still not sure of what we were dealing with, we went home and decided to wait about contacting the family until we knew something definite that we could share with them.

The next day we nervously went to see the doctor. By now I had convinced myself that this was all a huge mistake and that the physician had made a mistake. Again I told myself that *my wife couldn't possibly have breast cancer.* In the doctor's office my wife was examined and then the doctor showed us the mammogram. He explained that it was suspicious. He wanted to do a procedure called needle aspiration. This involves piercing the breast with a long needle and extracting a small sample of the lump. That sample is then examined by experts who confirm whether the sample is cancerous or benign. I decided to wait outside for that procedure.

We went home that afternoon and talked about the situation. Both of us were in a state of denial which fed off each other in a sort of symbiosis. We had convinced ourselves that this was all a big mistake and that the greedy doctors were just milking our insurance. I'm ashamed to admit that reaction, but it's the truth and just goes to show you the desperation of our denial. Let me state here and now for the record that every member of the medical community involved in my wife's treatment were kind-hearted professionals who never did anything but their best for her.

We returned to see the doctor after the results were in from the needle aspiration. It was now confirmed that my wife had breast cancer and the doctor laid out her options patiently and as kindly as possible. I remember the nails of her hand digging into my palm as I held her hand while we listened. When he finished speaking I realized that I must have missed something and looked at him as I asked him to repeat the question.

"I was asking which option you wanted to pursue," the doctor replied kindly.

I had to say, "I'm sorry Doctor, but I don't think we really absorbed all of that. Would you mind explaining it again?" To his credit the doctor kindly repeated my wife's options without a trace of irritation over our lack of concentration.

When he finished I looked to my wife but she shook her head and said, "I don't want to decide this right now."

I didn't think it good to put off the decision because the doctor had indicated that the cancer was the rapid-spreading variety and I would have pressed her like a fool. The doctor, seeing this, interceded and prevented me from interfering when he said that she didn't have to decide then and there. He scheduled an appointment to see her in two days and we left.

That night we sat discussing my wife's options. She could opt for a double mastectomy, a single mastectomy of the affected breast, or a lumpectomy that would remove the cancer and a small amount of healthy tissue surrounding the lump. I'm afraid I wasn't very useful in that conversation. I was terrified that I would give the wrong advice so when she asked me I simply told her that it was her decision to make and explained the options to her one by one. This was necessary because in the shock of everything that had happened, her mind seemed to be dumping the information much as my own had earlier in the day at the doctor's office.

The double mastectomy would insure that she never had a recurrence of breast cancer. The single mastectomy would insure that she never had a recurrence in the affected breast. The lumpectomy would remove the cancer and would be followed by chemotherapy and then radiation therapy, however there would be a chance of recurrence. After explaining her options I told her that my only goal was her continued presence in my life. I would support any decision that she made as long as the decision involved her getting well.

She eliminated the double mastectomy as too extensive at that point and we then discussed the remaining options again. After a lengthy discussion she decided that she wanted to go with the lumpectomy and follow-up treatments. I supported her decision because the doctor had assured us that if she opted for that procedure and there was a recurrence, her odds would be the same as the odds she was currently facing.

That night we broke the news to our respective families, both of which were shocked to hear that my wife was now battling the disease. Everyone was very supportive and kind. I explained the options when my wife faltered and handed me the phone. Some family members questioned the wisdom of the option that she had selected, but I defended her choice pointing out what the doctor had said regarding the odds. I also used an analogy by pointing out that if I had an injured finger I'd want it amputated and not the entire hand, so I could understand my wife's position.

No one actually said it, but I had a sense that perhaps they thought I had persuaded her to take an option that would retain the greater portion of the affected breast. That bothered me a little but I knew that simply wasn't the case. I would have accepted her decision for the double mastectomy because it wasn't her figure I was concerned about. My concern was that I would lose my wife and that thought was terrifying. Compared to that loss anything was preferable. But rationally I could relate to her desire to preserve as much of her body as possible.

The day my wife had her lumpectomy we were both overwhelmed by the support of the family members who were in attendance and sat in the large waiting room while she underwent the surgery. It wasn't just our immediate family either. Some of my aunts were there as was my stepfather's sister. I can't overemphasize the importance of the moral support and what it meant to me as the time dragged by in that waiting room. The doctor had informed us that they would do the lumpectomy and then do an axillary lymph node dissection.

When the doctor finally came to the waiting room to see me I was a nervous wreck. He informed me that my wife had come through the surgery just fine and was in recovery where she would remain for a while under the careful observation of the staff before being taken to her room. Then the doctor gave me the bad news. Several of the lymph nodes showed evidence that the cancer had spread. My wife had the fast spreading invasive cancer.

If not for the support of our families I don't know how I would have gotten past the next hour. My wife's oldest sister stepped forward and asked all the right questions as my mind reeled in shock from the news. She then patiently explained to me what the next steps would entail as my mind had stopped registering the doctor's words at some point.

When my wife was wheeled out of recovery I walked beside her bed and held her hand as she was wheeled through the halls. Flowers had arrived in her room while she was in surgery. The people at her factory had chipped in and sent a nice bouquet and an eloquent card that expressed their support for my wife. I remember that she cried as she read the card.

Then the moment I had dreaded finally came and my wife asked me what the doctor had said. Some of the family members had suggested that I keep the truth from her for at least a while. I even considered doing so, but as she looked into my eyes I could tell that she saw the truth in my face and in my eyes. We've always had an honest relationship and had been married for years at that point in time. I told her the truth at that point and she cried again. Her oldest sister once more proved an invaluable ally as she reassured my wife that this wasn't a death sentence. The doctor was fairly certain that the cancer had not spread beyond the lymph nodes.

The nurses in the hospital were wonderful during my wife's overnight stay. One of the nurses taught me how to strip the drain tube attached to my wife's breast to prevent it from stopping up. This was my first experience at assisting personally in my wife's medical care. There would be several more instances.

The second day of my wife's recovery the factory where she worked telephoned our home. There were some forms that I needed to pick up to fill out for Sue's medical leave. On the way to pick up those forms and turn in my wife's work uniforms, I stopped at a market and purchased a thank you card. Into that card I inserted a typed letter explaining to the people just how their thoughtful gift of flowers and the card had lifted Sue's spirits. And indeed that was true, for the tears she'd shed when reading the card were from a sense of joy and awe that her coworkers held her in such high esteem.

The receptionist in the factory asked me to wait while she went to get the personnel manager. The personnel manager was a warm and friendly lady who immediately inquired as to my wife's condition. I told the lady that she was on the mend but that she was still in a great deal of discomfort from the surgery. She gave me the papers that would have to be signed and filled out. She had gone to the trouble of filling out most of the paperwork for us. I thanked her for her kindness and the card and flowers.

I then gave the personnel manager the card which she read and handed to the receptionist to read as she read the letter which I had enclosed. Her eyes clouded with tears as she read the letter and I knew she'd reached the point where I'd described the moment of joy their thoughtful gift had brought to an otherwise gloomy day. She shared the letter with the receptionist who reacted in similar fashion.

I thanked them both and asked that they inform my wife's coworkers as to her condition and her gratitude for their thoughtfulness. I reference this incident because it was an awakening of awareness for both my wife and myself. Neither of us really understood the esteem with which our friends, family and coworkers held us until that week. It was a moving experience which helped reinforce in our minds that we were not so alone and alienated from our friends and families as we had first thought would be the case as we battled the disease.

A week after the surgery my wife visited her surgeon for a follow-up appointment. It was at this meeting that the surgeon told us he had good news. The cancer was hormone-receptive and therefore he recommended *hormonal therapy*. Of course I had no idea what this meant and he had to explain it all. He recommended Tamoxifen to be taken for five years after the chemotherapy course was completed. The doctor assured us that this was very good news as it is easier to prevent a recurrence of a hormone-receptive cancer. He also scheduled my wife for her first appointment with the oncologist in the neighboring city of Huntsville, Alabama.

Our first trip into the Huntsville oncology facility was simply amazing. To this day I can't forget the quality of the professionals who work in that section of the medical community. The doctor was great, but the protocol nurse was simply an angel. Indeed the entire staff worked diligently to treat patients who are more frightened than they have ever been in their lives, and on that score we were no exception. Their approach in my wife's case was to calmly work us through everything step by step.

The protocol nurse advised her that she might want to look into a turban or wig, as the chemotherapy treatments which she would be taking were strong and the treatments would cause hair loss. A week later we returned to oncology for my wife's first chemotherapy session. We'd heard all of the horror stories about how sick these treatments make the patients and it was with a great sense of dread that my wife took her first treatment which was administered via IV.

I remember trying to cheer her up by talking quietly to her as the small IV bag dripped the medication into her body. I even managed to make another patient smile as I told my wife a joke I'd recently heard and saved to use upon that otherwise solemn occasion. It's funny, some of the little things I remember.

We were greatly encouraged in the days following that first chemotherapy session. Though my wife felt a bit queasy, there was none of the debilitating sickness that we'd heard so much about. We had yet to learn that the chemotherapy would have a cumulative affect and the sickness would get geometrically worse with each successive treatment. Soon enough we would experience that reality check.

During this period of time my wife's sisters and nieces were a Godsend. They came to our home to help out in a major way with deep cleaning everything in the place. This was necessary because of the breakdown of a patient's immune system after losing so many lymph nodes and taking chemotherapy. Everything has to be as sanitary as humanly possible. Never being the greatest of house cleaners, I did what I could after work of course, but my efforts were terribly inadequate to our needs for perfection. My sister and mother also helped with the cleaning and often brought in meals as did my wife's sisters to insure that we had decent food while I experimented and learned to cook acceptable food. My wife had gone from surgical recovery to chemotherapy and was weak. None of us wanted her attempting housework or cooking if it was preventable.

During this time frame I also learned to do the shopping and do it right. This was a duty that my wife had always considered her domain and I seldom ventured into a grocery store for more than a handful of items. I didn't know where anything was and had to learn everything. I also learned to wash and dry the clothes and of course put everything away. These were tasks she normally took care of, but I found them pleasant and to this day still do the washing and drying, but she puts the clothes away citing that I never have learned to do this task to her satisfaction.

We continued to make the trips to Huntsville oncology every two weeks for the treatments and with each successive treatment the side effects grew progressively worse. As I recall it was just before the third chemotherapy treatment that my wife's hair began to fall out. Two days later I shaved her head. She cried as I cut her lovely hair down to the scalp in preparation for the shaving. With an aching heart, I assured her that it would come back. When we finished with her I shaved my own head in moral support and then our fifteen-year-old son volunteered to make it unanimous and his support was strictly unsolicited.

We had purchased a wig through a beauty shop just a quarter mile down the road from our home. The beautician was a kind hearted woman and is a family friend. She got the wig for us at her cost. My wife wore the wig out in public but preferred a turban when she was home.

Soon after this incident the chemotherapy side effects that we'd thought weren't going to be so bad got much, much worse. My wife would be incredibly sick the first and second nights after a session. Neither of us got much sleep at night and I can still to this day close my eyes and hear her groans of misery. Perhaps this is why to this day if she is down with a cold and groans at night I immediately awaken and check on her.

Sue began to complain of a foul smell emanating from her skin but I assured her that I smelled nothing unusual. At first I couldn't detect the odor she was referencing, but that soon changed. I never did tell her that there was a bad odor associated with the chemotherapy. She was miserable enough without thinking that her odor could offend people. It never offended me of course. I understood the source of the odor and that was frankly one worry she could do without. It is worth noting that our fifteen-year-old son did reference an odor once in her presence. As my wife looked at him I shook my head, gesturing for him to be quiet and blamed the odor on my cooking, which come to think of it, might well have been the source of what he smelled.

After the first few chemotherapy sessions my wife's surgeon recommended that she have a shunt embedded in her chest for the administering of the medication. This was necessary because the powerful drug was literally damaging her veins through which the chemotherapy was being administered. The surgery to implant this device in my wife's upper chest region seemed to be harder on her than the original surgery. The recuperation also seemed to be more difficult for her.

At around the midpoint of my wife's chemotherapy I began to run low on my remaining vacation days. I had managed to use them carefully by working most days and taking vacation days only the first two days after the chemotherapy and of course in the aftermath of the surgeries. Our brother-in-law who was married to my wife's sister understood the situation and he stepped forward volunteering to take my wife to the doctor's appointments and for chemo-therapy, thus allowing me to work and keep ends met to a degree. Our bill structure was pretty much tied to a dual income and with the loss of my wife's income things were beginning to get tough. My parents helped by waiving one of the house payments on the home we'd bought from them.

With my brother-in-law stepping in to assist, I managed to keep us afloat some-how. Once more the assistance of our fami-lies was a Godsend. It seemed every time they visited they brought in groceries and household cleaning supplies. Sue's oldest sister, Carolyn, and the one next to my wife in age named Christine were fantastic. God bless them for their kindness. I will never forget what they did for us and would do anything for either of them. Christine is the mother of the nieces who helped with the cleaning and the wife of the brother-in-law who was himself a cancer survivor. His moral support for us was incredibly beneficial. He was without a doubt the kindest, most un-selfish and giving man I've ever known. Sadly the disease came back in his case and he passed away a few years back. My wife never forgot his kindness and would visit him to try to cheer him up and lend her moral support. She was devastated when he passed away. Everyone who knew that gentleman was devastated.

There were a battery of other medical tests from CT scans and an MRI to x-rays and blood work. My brother-in-law took my wife to many of these tests so that I could continue to save as much time off as possible. These tests were necessary to determine if the cancer had spread to other organs.

The last two chemotherapy sessions were by far the worst. My wife had a total of eight of these treatments but after the seventh I was not at all certain she would take the final treatment. She was tired of being so sick and miserable after the treatments and was ready to say enough. This turn of events terrified me because we had been assured that if she took all of the treatments and medications then there was a good chance of affecting a cure.

Yet at the height of her sickness after the treatment she was adamant that the seventh would be the last. Fortunately, she had a change of heart as she got better after a few days. The last chemotherapy after effects were devastating. I lost track of the times that she threw up and getting her to eat anything at all was very difficult. I couldn't even tempt her with the popsicles which had comforted her after several of the treatments.

A few days after that final treatment we got a call from oncology. My wife's white blood cell count was down and they needed us to come in for a supply of injections which I was to give her daily to build her blood back up.

We were on Church Street, about a quarter mile from the oncology building when a wave of sickness hit my wife and she asked me to pull over so that she could throw up. I immediately slowed and was looking for a place to pull off the road, but before I could stop she threw open her door and leaned precariously out to vomit. I grabbed her by the arm to keep her from falling out of the car as I brought it to a stop. In the rearview mirror I saw a police squad car and figured they'd stop but they just drove around us.

In the oncology facility one of the nurses patiently worked with me to teach me step by step how I was to administer the premeasured injections, then under her supervision I gave my wife her first injection of this drug. I think giving her that first injection is probably one of the hardest things I had to do during her treatment phase. The absolute last thing I wanted to do was cause my wife pain or discomfort but you do what you have to do for those you love. Someone had to give her the injections and at least if I stepped up and took care of that she could have them at home where she was most comfortable. I was able to do what was required though I never did get over the paranoia regarding breaking a needle. Thank goodness that never happened. We were both greatly relieved the day that I gave her the last injection.

In the aftermath of the chemotherapy there came a brief period of time of recuperation and then the radiation therapy began. I took her to the first and the afore-mentioned brother-in-law took her to several. By now I had used all of my available vacation and my personnel manager had me take family medical leave for the time needed to take care of my wife after her last surgery. The last surgery that my wife had was the one to have the embedded shunt removed. The surgery was hard on her. The recuperation took longer than her original surgery or so it seemed to me.

Through all of this our families were supportive and I don't see how we could have gotten through it without them. I think a special bond formed between myself and my wife's family during this ordeal. I believe a deep mutual respect developed. Deeper than the normal respect. The same is true for the relationship that my wife has with my family, all of whom were as stricken by stark fear as was I when I first learned of my wife's cancer.

Sue resisted all efforts on the part of the medical community to get her into a support group because no support groups included the spouses. I encouraged her to go and not worry about me, but she was adamant that outside the medical community, I had been her caregiver and most closely shared her experiences. She insisted that together we would get through the aftermath just as we had faced the ordeal. With strong family support this was possible for us. In her thinking we already had a support group. One which didn't exclude the spouse and had been there for her from day one. This is not meant to be a criticism of support groups. They do great work. I reference it only because the spousal exclusion was the reason that my wife never officially joined a support group. I wish she had done so. I'm sure that there were things that such a group would have been able to assist her with when it comes to dealing with issues related to breast cancer. But my wife had been through so much that I was unwilling to press the issue.

Then the Tamoxifen hormonal pill treatments began. Tamoxifen has several side effects but the one that was most notable in my wife's case were the wild mood swings. The first two years were the worst. It got bad a few times but I do not regret those times. She was taking a medication that could prevent a recurrence and possibly save her life. Therefore any inconvenience for myself and our son was tolerated good-naturedly because we knew it was the medication causing the mood swings and she is more than worth a few sharp comments. I mention this as a caution to men whose wives are taking that medication. If they suffer mood swings then always remember it's the medication causing this. Be patient. I promise that phase *won't last.*

Early detection is the key to surviving breast cancer.

It is possible to survive breast cancer. The key to survival is early detection. To that end I cannot stress enough the importance of learning the early detection techniques. There are a multitude of sources out there from which you can gather this information. So learn the warning signs. Husbands, you need to learn the warning signs as well. One of the signs is a bloody discharge from the breast. Husbands may be the first to note that warning sign. Therefore if you are a husband you should educate yourself in these matters.

~

Ricky Sides was Born in Florence, Alabama, in May of 1958. The author's writing experience includes the science fiction, action adventure book *The Birth of the Peacekeepers* and the other books in the series. The author also wrote the fantasy, action adventure *Brimstone and the Companions of Althea* series which is a nine novel set, based on the on-line game t4c (the fourth coming) and was written by Ricky Sides under the pen name Raistlin and edited and collaborated on by a wonderful lady from Louisiana under the pen name Kittie Justice. The author also wrote a book on women's self-defense named *The Ultimate in Women's Self-Defense*.

Ricky Sides
rsides22219@charter.net
http://www.sonofartherk.com

The Last Step
Michael E. Thompson

John Mallory shivered slightly as he stepped out into the cold autumn morning. The air had that crisp quality that lets you know that winter can't be far off. "I should have worn my coat," John said to himself. "Oh well, it won't matter for long."

"What a view," John thought as he looked around. He could see the bay from his vantage point and the Golden Gate Bridge. He could hear the sounds of traffic and off in the distance a church bell was ringing. John shivered again as he stepped forward.

*

"Bang! I got you, Johnny!" Pete yelled, stepping from behind the tree with his cowboy pistol in his hand.

"You missed me! Bang! Bang! I got you!" Johnny yelled from behind the car.

"No way! You cheated! I got you first."

"You did not."

"I did too. Shot you right in the head."

"Did not!"

"Did too!"

"Johnny! Time for dinner!" Johnny's mother called from the front porch. "Come in and get washed up."

"Aw, mom! Do I have to?"

"Yes, you do. Now get in here."

"Can Pete stay for dinner?"

"Well, I suppose so if it's okay with his mother."

"Come on, Pete, let's call your mom. Race you!"

*

"Did you get them, John?" Pete asked as John ran up.

"Yeah, they're in my pocket," John replied, looking over his shoulder. "Let's go down by the pond," John said, leading the way down the path. Twenty minutes later they were sitting on a large rock beside a small pond. The woods around them were alive with the sounds of crickets.

Pete, slapping at a mosquito, asked, "Can I see them now?"

"Sure," John replied, reaching into his pocket he withdrew a small plastic bag with a pack of cigarettes and a book of matches.

"You sure your mom won't miss these?" Pete asked.

"No, she always has a couple of cartons opened up around the house. She'll never miss one pack." John peeled the plastic from the pack and tore open the paper underneath, and shook out two cigarettes, handing one to Pete. He opened the matches and struck it against the gritty strip. He held it up for Pete to light his cigarette, and then lit his own. He inhaled the acrid smoke only to start coughing violently. Across from him Pete was also coughing. John tried to inhale from the cigarette again as his coughing subsided. By the time the cigarette was burned halfway through, John was beginning to feel nauseous. Looking up, he noticed that Pete looked a little green.

"Maybe this wasn't such a good idea," Pete said.

*

"Oh, John! It's beautiful," Kate cried out as she looked at the purple orchid wrist corsage. "It goes perfectly with my dress." She held out her left hand as John slipped it around her wrist.

"It sure does." John sighed as he looked at Kate's dress. It was lavender with spaghetti straps and he thought she was the most beautiful thing he had ever seen.

"All right now. You two stand over here and let me take a few pictures." Kate's mother pointed to a spot against the living room wall.

"Mother, we don't have time for that now."

"You can spare a few minutes for a picture. After all, this isn't just any dance, it's your Senior Prom and I want pictures. Now, if you please."

Kate smiled as she moved to the spot her mother indicated. "Come on, John. If we don't humor her she'll never let us out of here." She took John's hand as he stood beside her.

"Smile now!" Kate's mother said as she raised the camera up to shoot.

*

"You know if you faint or throw up out there I'm sending the tape to *America's Funniest Videos*," Pete chuckled. "Who knows, I could win the big money!"

"Just shut up and help me with this damned thing," John said, taking his hands away from the limp bow tie around his neck. "If I do throw up it'll be your fault."

"Hey, nobody forced you to do that many shooters last night. I wish I could have gotten a picture of the look on your face when the stripper showed up," Pete laughed as he stood in front of John and started working on the bow tie.

"Let's just not ever mention last night again, especially when Kate is around. If she ever finds out she'll kill us both."

"Look, all you did was let a mostly naked woman sit in your lap," Pete said with a smirk. "A stripper is traditional for a bachelor party, and what kind of best man would I be if I broke with tradition? There, that's got it." Pete stepped back and pointed to the mirror on the wall. "You look fine."

John looked at his reflection in the mirror. "Still, let's just keep the stripper a secret all right?"

"That could be a little difficult since I uploaded the pictures to my web page this morning," Pete grinned.

"You what!"

"Just kidding. But I may have to blackmail you for them later."

They both turned at the sound of the door behind them opening. They could hear the organ music clearly as John's father stepped into the room. "It's time son."

John felt a slight wave of nerves as they stepped into the church and walked over to take their places in front of Father Flannigan. The organ music changed to the Wedding March as everyone stood and turned to look down the aisle toward the back as the flower girl turned the corner at the front of the procession.

*

"Damn you! I'll never let you touch me again you bastard!" Kate groaned as she crushed John's left hand with hers. Sweat was dripping from her hair as she grimaced in pain. Looking down between her spread legs, she pleaded with the man standing there. "Please! I'll give you anything you want. Can't I just have something, an epidural, or morphine, anything?"

"It's too late for that now, you're crowning," the doctor replied. "Now, push!"

"I can't push anymore! It hurts too much."

"Come on, Kate! You can do this! Just a few more pushes!" John encouraged.

"I can't! It hurts too much!"

"Kate, you have to push! Now push!"

Kate gritted her teeth, took a deep breath, and pushed hard. "Aaaaargh!!!"

"That's it! Here comes the head!"

*

"Daddy!" The little girl squealed as she ran into John's arms. He scooped her up and held her high in the air.

"How's my Jennifer doing today?" he asked, giving her a noisy wet kiss on the cheek.

"Stop it, Daddy, that tickles." Jennifer pushed John's face away with her hands. "I thought Mommy was picking me up from daycare today."

"She has to work late so I'm afraid you're stuck with me for dinner."

"Can we go to McDonald's?"

"You know Mommy doesn't like it when eat fast food."

"We don't have to tell her, do we?" Jennifer smiled.

"It'll be our secret."

*

"Mr. Mallory, these officers are here to see you," said John's secretary from the doorway of his office. "They said it was important." John looked up as two police officers entered his office and walked over towards his desk.

"Are you John Mallory?"

"Yes, I am, officer," John said, standing. "What's this all about?"

"I am sorry to have to tell you this but your wife and daughter have been involved in a serious accident."

"Oh my God. Are they all right? What happened?"

"It appears that the brakes failed on a delivery truck, causing it to hit your wife's car broadside. I am sorry, sir, but your wife was killed instantly."

John's body went numb as he sagged back into his chair.

"What - What about Jennifer, my daughter?"

"I don't know her condition, sir; she was taken to San Francisco Memorial by helicopter."

"I - I have to get there."

*

"I am very sorry, Mr. Mallory, but she has severe damage to her brain. It's a miracle that she's even alive."

"But she will recover, won't she?" John asked, looking through the intensive care window to where his daughter lay with so many tubes and lines, her small body so battered that she was unrecognizable.

"No, Mr. Mallory, I'm afraid you don't understand. There is nothing else we can do for her now. She's brain dead."

*

Through a fog John heard a sound. Then the sound went away. In moments the sound returned. John lifted his pounding head from the pillow, knocking over an empty whiskey bottle as he fumbled to pick up the phone. He finally got the phone to his ear.

"Hello, hello?"

"John, where are you? The meeting with the client starts in ten minutes. We need your report. John? John, are you there? John!"

Letting the receiver fall to the floor, John laid his head back down on the pillow as his eyes closed.

*

"You wanted to see me, Mr. Peterson?"

"Yes, John, come in and have a seat. I don't know how to say this other than to just come out a say it. John, I know things have been difficult for you since the accident. Everyone here at the firm has tried to be understanding, but it's been almost a year and you're not getting any better. You're constantly late, if you show up at all. You're obviously drinking too much. John, you need professional help."

"Mr. Peterson, I know I've had problems but I assure you that I will..."

"Stop, John. I can't listen to any more of your excuses. We're letting you go. If you get the help you need there may be a place for you here again someday, but for now I must ask you to clean out your desk by the end of the day. I am sorry, John."

*

"Officer, keep those people back," Steve Montgomery said, pulling rubber gloves onto his hands. He turned to the grisly scene in front of him. "You know, Terry, even after fourteen years you never get used to this."

"I know what you mean," Detective Terry Summers replied looking high up over his head. "What is that about, 18 stories?"

"Something like that, maybe 20. It sure is a hell of a long way down." He carefully inserted his gloved hand into the body's suit coat pocket and removed the wallet. "Driver's license says this is John Mallory, age 28. His address is only about twenty minutes from here."

"Maybe he worked in this building."

"You ever wonder what goes through their heads on the way down?"

"They say your whole life flashes before your eyes right before you die. But who knows? The coroner should be here shortly to take the body."

Mike Thompson, retired USAF Major, is a certified registered nurse anesthetist living in Northern California with his wife and two cats. He is not, he reminds the world, a writer, just a guy with a story to tell.

Visit him online at http://ised8u.blogspot.com.

Cat Feathers
Brendan Carroll

When I arrived home from work yesterday, tired and feeling somewhat grumpy from a long, unproductive day trying to pound conformity pegs into solid blocks of disestablishmentarianism, I found a rather wrinkly piece of yellow legal paper folded up and stuffed under the edge of my computer monitor pedestal. I sat down at the desk with a tall glass of iced tea and very carefully removed the paper, reluctant to see what might be written on it. I knew that something was written on it simply due to the fact that it had been so cleverly placed right where I would see it and because it had not been there earlier in the day when I left for work. I say I was reluctant because such notes, similar to phone calls in the dead of night, are not usually good news. In fact, I think I actually closed my eyes when I opened it, hoping one last time that nothing would be there when I opened them except uniform blue lines. After a few seconds, I ventured a quick look and was not surprised to see ink blots, splotches and paw prints on the page. Yes, that's right... *paw prints* on the page. Filled with apprehension, I quickly looked around and found a blotchy, black spot on the carpet and the remains of a Pilot-G2 C7 ballpoint pen, one of my favorite writing tools scattered around the stain.

Returning my attention to the messy epistle, I scanned the page and sure enough, just as I feared, it was signed simply: *the Puglet.*

It was not the first such letter I had received from *the Puglet.* Most people would scoff and say that I am imagining things or just plain crazy. Pugs would never use a ballpoint pen to write a letter. I know that it sounds incredible, since Pugs normally use felt tip markers when they write, but my Puglet is different. She writes only with Pilot-G2s and then she proceeds to destroy them so that no one can ever use them again. Some sort of religious ritual it would seem.

Another thing that most people do not know about Pugs: they are extremely devout and practice many rituals. Of course many of these rituals are obscure and not readily recognized by the layman. Pug initiates, on the other hand, will recognize them right away. The subtle meditational snore, for instance, may simply appear to be a Pug sleeping with his/her eyes open, but this is not so. Not at all. It is part of the Ancient and Accepted Chinese Rite wherein the Pug goes into a deep meditational trance, eyes wide open and alert for any scraps of food that may fall from the laps of nearby humans.

But enough about that. The tattered paper indicated that she was lodging yet another complaint about the terms of our Pugmaster Accord wherein she is required to vacate my chair when I come home. Now these Accords are not to be taken lightly and date back to the first Pugmaster Accord signed in 1078 CE and more commonly known as the Magna Pugna. In compliance with our Accord, she normally jumps down and meets me at the door, barking, howling and making use of all sorts of exclusive Pug noises in order to let me know that her bowl is empty, she wants to go outside and/or she needs a new treat to chew on as if I would not already be aware of these things. The particulars of this issue are covered in Chapter Two, paragraph 3, subparagraph b wherein I am obliged to see to her basic needs before doing absolutely anything else up to and including putting down bags of groceries or other items I might be carrying at the time. This requirement sometimes becomes a bit difficult to satisfy and I would have negotiated a bit more leeway concerning the time constraints involved had I realized the magnitude of the problems inherent with compliance in regard to subparagraph b.

Nevertheless, Chapter 2, paragraph 3, subparagraph b was not her major concern yesterday afternoon. It was Chapter Three, paragraph 2, subparagraph g that had her knickers in a knot. The stipulation that requires her to vacate my chair promptly upon my arrival is completely unnecessary in her opinion. Since I must comply with paragraph 3, subparagraph b immediately upon arrival, she felt that I have been cheating her out of another two to three minutes of free chair time. In other words, she does not see the need to evacuate the chair until I actually open the patio door in anticipation of her needs. According to her complaint, she could quite easily bark, growl and howl from the comfort of my chair rather than meeting me at the door. As I was eschewing the merits of her written complaint, I noticed that she was not in the room with me which was highly unusual since, as I said before, she normally meets me at the door whenever I come home.

I got up and went in search of her, thinking that I needed to discuss her complaint with her in person... er... in canine... er...

whatever. I wanted to remind her that she could not possibly convey her needs with any semblance of accuracy from my chair, which is fairly far removed from the door I use when I come home. Furthermore, she cannot actually see the patio doors if she is sitting in my chair, hence she would not really know whether I had opened the door for her. Thinking it odd that she was not sitting in front of me, frowning, tilting her head back and forth quizzically, I got up wearily and looked for her in the bedroom, the bathroom, the spare bedroom and the kitchen. I even went outside and checked the backyard and the storage shed in mounting panic, thinking that perhaps I had left her outside while I was gone.

Strange, I thought. *Where could she be?*

Retracing my steps, I searched again more slowly, calling her name in that special playful tone that usually brings her running every time, but all to no avail. I went back to my bedroom and walked around the bed dejectedly to get the phone. I would have to call the neighbors and learn whether anyone had seen her. I would have to make posters to tack on the neighborhood light poles: *Missing Puglet!* I would have to find pictures of her and make posters of them and leave my phone number for complete strangers to access. And then sit home, waiting to sort through the calls, many of which would be from my neighbors using thinly disguised voices congratulating me on finally losing the annoying little dog with the smashed face.

The horror of all these terrible things going through my mind could only be matched and displaced by the horror of suddenly finding my favorite feather pillow, disemboweled and flat on the floor. Tiny goose feathers were everywhere! Suspicious of foul play, I turned slowly and looked at my bed, wondering why I had not noticed the missing pillow the first time I had checked the bedroom. The spread appeared unruffled, replete with an illusory feather pillow tucked under the covers at the head of the bed.

Cautiously, I reached out and placed my hand on the lump where my feather pillow should have been and it moved.

Aha! The missing Pug! I thought, but I was wrong. It was the neighbor's cat!

Turned out, my Puglet was hiding in the linen closet. The cat quickly gave up this information when threatened with a bath. Turns out the Puglet had paid the kitty to impersonate the pillow in an attempt to trick me. Furthermore, the letter was nothing more than a fake, a first strike employed in an effort to distract me by throwing up a smokescreen. The Puglet has been known for clever ruses such as this.

When all was said and done, the Puglet

spent the night in the backyard while the kitty pretended to be my pillow. It was a bit touch and go at first, but once I had the pillow sham over her head, it was all downhill.

Brendan Carroll currently resides in the Texas Hill Country and works as a public servant for the State of Texas. He has been writing fiction for over thirty years and has written thirty-five novels. His most recent publications are currently available in Kindle ebook format at Amazon.com including Books 1-14 of the Red Cross of Gold series. *The Red Cross of Gold* series chronicles the adventures of a semi-immortal Templar Knight who's clandestine Order of the Red Cross of Gold has survived since the Holy Crusades. Books I-V are also available in POD from Amazon.com in paperback.

Also available is *Tempo Rubato*, a fictional novel and tribute to Wolfgang Amadeus Mozart.

Brendan can be found at Kindlboards.com and at his blog site on Blogspot: http://redcrossofgold.blogspot.com/ and at Wordpress: http://brendancarroll.wordpress.com/. He is also listed at Author's Den.

Pound of Flesh
Richard Gerard

One

It was Wednesday night, and Billy Thompson was on the prowl. His wife Anne was fifty miles away, two towns over, waiting for him. Missing him. He had called earlier and told her that he had to go out of town on business. It was an emergency, and couldn't be helped. Anne prayed for her husband's safety as a massive thunderstorm pounded the night sky. She hoped he was okay.

Billy was more than okay. He was doing great. He had hit it off with a beautiful woman named Beth, and after a few drinks, accepted her invitation back to her place. Neither got much sleep that night, and both called in sick Thursday morning. They continued their escapade until both were too tired to move. Billy called his wife and told her the problem was getting worse. He wouldn't be home until tomorrow.

Billy and Beth finally fell asleep entwined together. They woke up that evening and proceeded to paint the town red, dancing the night away. After another night at her place, Billy left Beth to return to his wife. He had her number, and promised to make it back this way as soon as he could.

Billy made it home before his wife had gotten off of work. After washing away any evidence in the shower and washing machine, Billy called Anne to tell her he was home.

"Hey baby. I finally made it home, and I missed you so much. I'm grilling up dinner, so don't be late. I love you."

After their goodbyes, Billy headed outside to fire up the grill. Even after the past two days, Billy was feeling amorous. After a wonderful steak dinner, Billy and Anne retired to the bedroom for a little personal welcome home.

Billy spent all of Saturday in bed. He hadn't gotten much sleep the past few days, and had a lot of catching up to do. His ever-doting wife catered to his every need and whim, hoping he had not caught that swine flu thing that had been in the news recently. By Sunday, Billy said he felt better, and he and Anne went out to the movies. Everything was right with Anne's little piece of the world.

Billy and Anne returned to work Monday morning. Anne was a little worried about her friend Beth, who had called in sick on Thursday and Friday. Anne had meant to call her over the weekend to check on her, but she spent all day Saturday taking care of Billy, and she forgot. Anne felt like a crap friend. Beth came in looking vibrant. Anne apologized for not calling and checking on her, but Beth put her at ease.

"Don't worry about it sweetie. I probably wouldn't have picked up the phone anyway. I met this guy Bill at a bar on Wednesday night, and boy did we hit it off. He was a stud, Anne. My God, I wish you could have seen us going at it. He didn't leave my house until Friday morning; said he had to get back to work."

Beth went on to describe everything they had done in intimate detail. She was wrapping up the story ten minutes later.

"Oh, Anne, I almost forgot the best part. He had this perverted tattoo down there. It was a pair of red lips circling his member, like he was telling me what to do, and I did it. I kissed those painted lips repeatedly, and he loved it. He said something like the last woman he was with couldn't go all the way down, but I took care of him. God I'm such a slut. I hope he calls me."

With a wave, Beth left Anne for her own cubicle. Anne was dumbstruck as the reality sank it. Her husband Billy had a tattoo like that. As she worked out the timeline in her head, her anger was starting to flair. Before her temper got out of hand, Anne decided that revenge was going to be the best solution to the problem. She wasn't really mad at Beth because she had no way of knowing who her new friend was. Anne didn't have any pictures of Billy in her cubicle, and Beth had never seen them together. Anne decided Billy was entirely to blame and spent the rest of the day scheming. By the end of the day, she had a working idea in her mind. It would take some planning, but Anne was confident she could pull it off. Anne made sure to say goodbye to Beth that afternoon. She would need to keep up appearances for some time before she could exact her pound of flesh.

Over the next few weeks, Anne started talking to Billy about wanting to go on vacation. It had been over a year since their last one, and she started mentioning places they could go. Billy didn't really listen, instead planning his own little getaway for the next week. When he told her that he was going to have to go out of town again, Anne wasn't surprised. While he was gone, she called his office pretending to be a client. She was told that Bill Thompson had a family emergency and wasn't in. She didn't leave a message.

When Billy returned home, Anne again played the dutiful wife, pretending that nothing was wrong. She continued on normally, still talking of a vacation. She told him that she wanted to go camping in the mountains for a week. As a child, she often went camping with her family, and she missed the adventure. Billy wasn't keen on the idea, but relented to his wife's wishes. Billy's idea of roughing it was having the cable go out, but Anne used all of her charms to convince him.

"Don't worry honey," Anne told him. "I'll plan everything. You just need to ask for a week off in April. I think spring would be the best time to go. It's not too hot or cold, and some of the plants should be flowering by then. It will be wonderful!"

Anne spent the next few months buying all of the supplies they would need. She hadn't been camping since they married. They didn't even own a tent. Billy, never suspecting his wife knew of his indiscretions, continued to play the field. He "worked late" every few weeks, and even made another "business trip" to see Beth.

On the first Saturday of their vacation, Anne was busy making sure that she had packed everything. She even had a detailed map of the area she wanted to spend the week in. She gave directions, while Billy drove. It only took three hours in the car before they arrived at the trail head. There were no other cars here this early in the season, and this place had never been busy even at peak times. To dissuade any would-be rescuers, Anne left a note in the car with their expected return date. She wanted to devote the entire week to Billy, without interruption. After loading up their packs, they headed off into the forest with Anne leading the way. She still recognized the area from her childhood.

Billy started complaining about an hour into their hike. Anne did her best to soothe him, promising the payoff was worth it. She described the beautiful but fictitious lake they were heading to, and what they were going to do in the tent once it was up. She even hinted at some lakeside action which kept Billy moving toward his reward.

After another few hours of hard hiking, she found a nice secluded spot that met her criteria and told Billy that she had to stop and use the bathroom. She dropped her pack and headed off for some privacy. Instead of using the bathroom, Anne circled around and came up behind Billy silently. With a powerful swing, Anne hit Billy in the back of the head with a rock. He dropped to the ground and didn't move. It was getting late, and Anne had a lot of work to do before dark.

Two

Billy awoke the next morning with a jolt. He was confused and disoriented, and couldn't understand why he was unable to move. His head throbbed, and it took him a moment to figure out he was lying on the forest floor, staked out, and naked. Billy started screaming, but the only animals he roused were a murder of crows. Billy hoped they weren't symbolic of things to come.

The last thing Billy remembered was hiking with his wife. The thought of her brought a fresh bout of screams to his lips. He had no idea where she was, or if she was okay. Billy continued screaming until he was hoarse, but it proved futile. No one came to his rescue. There was only one other soul within miles, and she wasn't going to let Billy go after all of her planning and hard work.

As the screams for help subsided, Anne decided it was time to go see her husband. She needed to talk to him and explain why she did this. Billy, with almost no voice left, tried yelling again as he heard approaching footsteps.

"Help. Help me," Billy cried softly.

As Anne entered his field of vision, relief washed over his face.

"Oh my God Anne. I'm so glad it's you. Let me loose. I don't know who did this, and they might come back. Quick. Untie me. Did you see anybody?"

Billy kept on rambling, but Anne had stopped walking and just stared, smiling.

"Anne, come on. Snap out of it and help me. Anne? . . . Anne?"

Billy stuttered to a stop, realizing that his wife wasn't going to help him. Slowly, a new realization crept over him.

"Anne? Did you do this to me?" Billy asked hesitantly.

Anne kept staring and smiling dreamily, before slowly sauntering over to Billy's feet.

"Hi Billy. Did you have a nice nap? I bet your head hurts. I had to use a rock to knock you out. I hope the cobwebs have cleared out by now. I want you fully aware."

Billy, coming to terms with the fact his wife had done this to him, could only ask why, and Anne freaked.

"Why, Billy? Why did I lead you out here, into the middle of nowhere? Why did I hit you on the head with a rock? Why did I stake you to the ground naked? Why? Why? I'll yell you why," Anne screamed incredulously. "I'll tell you why. Do you remember a woman named Beth? You met her in a bar back in January. You met her in a bar, and went back to her place, and fucked. You cheated on me Billy, while I sat at home alone, missing you. You were supposed to be on a business trip. You cheated on me Billy. She told me you two did it like bunnies. She told me you went down on her Billy. You did all of these things with another woman Billy, while I was home alone missing you. How could you, you bastard? How could you?

"I bet that Beth never told you where she worked, did she Billy? No, I know she didn't because if she did, you would have known that she works with me. She works with me Billy. She was my friend. She missed work for two days, and when she came back, I asked her if she was feeling better. I asked her that because she was my friend Billy. She said she called in sick to spend two days with a guy she met in a bar. With you Billy, she skipped work to be with you. She told me about the marathon sex, and all of the different things you tried. Do you know I listened to her for ten minutes, before I figured out she was talking about you. She recounted the events in detail, saving the best detail for last. You know that tattoo you got back in college Billy? The red lips you have down there? That's how I knew Billy. That's how I knew you cheated on me.

"I kept this bottled inside for months Billy. I planned this entire thing out, without letting anyone know. I didn't even tell her that her dream man was my husband. Do you know why Billy? Do you know why? I kept my mouth shut so no one would ever suspect that I killed you."

Anne let those words hang in the air, while Billy tried to find his voice. He decided to admit the affair and beg for forgiveness.

"Anne, I'm so sorry. That time I spent with her has haunted me all this time. I regretted doing that to you. I wanted to tell you about it, but I could never find the words. I didn't want you to leave me, Anne. I love you so much; I didn't want to lose you. Please Anne, please forgive me. It was just a one time thing, Anne. Please don't do anything you will regret later. Untie me Anne and I will do whatever you want to make it up to you. Please Anne, please."

Anne let the poor man finish digging his grave before continuing.

"You know Billy, that was a great speech," Anne applauded. "I would probably have believed that story, except for the fact that I know she wasn't the only one. I started checking up on you Billy. When you said you had to stay and work late, I would call. I would call Billy, but you were never there. When you had to go away on company business, I would call your office, Billy. I would pretend to be a client and call. No one at your office ever said you were away on business. They just said that you had called in with an excuse. You see Billy, I know Beth wasn't the only one. What I don't know, is how many others there were. How many were there Billy? How many others?"

Billy decided to roll the dice and deny any other affairs. He had his story and he had to stick with it.

"Anne, there was only the one, I swear. Only the one."

"You will tell me Billy. Before we are through, you will tell me everything."

Billy didn't like the finality in her tone, and started screaming for help again. Anne didn't care. She knew these woods were empty. Her early morning scouting trip verified that. Anne knew they were utterly alone, and she smiled.

While Billy continued to scream, Anne returned to her tent and started cooking lunch. She had pitched it about 30 yards away, just far enough away from him to not be kept awake by his begging and screaming. Anne ate a large lunch, not worrying about running low of supplies. They had packed enough for two, but Billy wouldn't need any more food. By the time she finished eating, Billy had gotten quiet again. His voice was gone. Anne returned to him, carrying two bottles.

"Have some water Billy. I'm sure your throat is raw from all that yelling."

She knelt down and slowly poured the cool, refreshing liquid into his mouth. Billy unconsciously thanked her before remembering that this was her doing. Anne hushed him, when he started yelling again.

"Billy, you are going to stop that screaming so I can talk to you. Okay?"

Billy quieted down, in the hopes of winning some sympathy.

"That's good Billy, that's good. Now we can have some fun."

Anne took the other bottle she was holding and smeared some peanut butter onto Billy's stomach.

"Billy, you can probably feel a few bugs and ants crawling on your body. I even see a few bites already. What you don't know is that I chose this spot where you are lying down very carefully. You see Billy, right below your crotch, between your knees, is a very large fire ant mound. Now your body is far enough away from it that they don't feel threatened right now, but watch this."

Anne picked up a nice-sized stick and started stirring the ground between Billy's legs. When she was satisfied, she gently laid the stick down so that one end of it was propped up on Billy's crotch. The other end was right in the middle of the now angry nest. As the first ants found Billy and bit down, he started screaming.

"Don't worry Billy," she cooed over his screams. "I brought along some of my EpiPens so you won't die from the toxins. I won't let you die from dehydration either. I'm going to stay right here nourishing your body, while your body nourishes those ants.

Your screams are going to sing me to sleep every night until you have been eaten alive."

With that, Anne went back to her tent and retrieved a hammock. She strung it between two trees about fifteen feet from Billy.

"Sing me a lullaby Billy. I want to take a nap."

Billy put his heart and soul into making that sweet music, as Anne swayed in the gentle breeze.

Epilogue

A lone woman rambles down a dirt path, headed for the highway. When a car finally stops, she asks for some water, and to call the cops. She tells the story of her and her husband going camping, before getting separated in the woods. She doesn't know where he is, and they need to search for him. Since she and Billy hiked so much, the searchers don't know where to look. His remains were never found. It was assumed that he died, and animals carted off the body in pieces. No one ever thought it was ant sized pieces. When Anne finally returns to work, Beth greets her with open arms, ever the friend.

Refusing to yield to the pressures of a single genre or style, Richard Gerard's poetry and short fiction provide a glimpse into the bottomless chasm where the fodder for his pen dwells. His latest jaunt into the abyss, *Pound of Flesh*, will take you on a fast ride into the psyche of a scorned woman and the revenge born of a strong mind. His other eclectic works include *Recycled Tomes* and *Angel of Death*.

Purgatory
Maria Rachel Hooley

I've often wondered if the reason I could never accept the Catholic faith was the idea of purgatory, that netherworld between Heaven and Hell. As I sit in this hospital waiting room, watching smoke spirals rising from my cigarette, I think I've found it. "He's dead," I say, trying to make myself believe it, but I can't seem to leave, or accept that I am no longer waiting for anything.

I should have been his mother or wife, but his mother had died years ago, and Jordan had never wanted a wife. The waiting room is empty at four a.m., not that anyone else would have come at a more respectable hour.

I close my eyes. In the darkness, where nothing breathes, I remember his face and

when I first realized we could never be together.

* * *

Jordan sat on his bed. "I'm not breaking up with you because I don't care. You're
wonderful, Amy."

I pressed my hands into my jeans.
"Then why? We've been together since high
school." I glanced at his class ring on my
finger. "You said we'd get married after college. It's only two more years."

He looked at the floor, starting to say
something, but stopping. "I can't pretend
anymore. I'm not attracted to you."

I winced. "What?" I brought my hand to
my forehead and sat on the sofa. "You don't
like the way I look? The way I dress?" A thick
lump settled in my throat.

"No," Jordan said. "It's not anything like
that." He took my hand in his and sat next
to me. His fingers softly skimmed my hand.
"You're a wonderful woman. Any guy in his
right mind would find you beautiful." He
brushed the hair from my face. "No matter
how much I care, I don't feel that way."

I leaned toward him, wanting more
words. Needing them. "I don't understand."

Jordan closed his eyes. "I'm gay."

"No, you're not!" I yelled. "It's a mistake!
It's all a mistake!" The words jumbled together. I cinched my fingers around his as
though that would allow me to keep him.

He shook his head. Slowly. "For a while I wasn't sure. Now I am."

I stood and backed away while wrapping my arms around my chest. "Why are you telling me this? Why didn't you just lie?"

He walked to the shelf holding all his football trophies. "You wouldn't have believed a lie, and I knew if anyone could understand, you would."

I watched the ceiling fan's slow spin. "What am I supposed to understand?"

He touched the golden figurines. "All my life I've tried to be someone I'm not. I've tried to be the perfect son, the perfect athlete. But I'm not any of those things." He snatched his fingers from the trophy. When he turned back, I saw traces of tears. "I feel like I owe you an explanation, Amy. But even that's not as simple as I thought."

"What is?" I asked, feeling my heart ramming my chest. "I thought loving you was easy. So easy it would last forever." I took off his ring and tried to hand it to him. My fingers wouldn't stop shaking.

He reached to wipe away the tears, but I ducked back, proffering the ring more firmly. He opened his palm and let the ring fall into it before closing his fingers. "I'm sorry," he said, finally. "I had to tell you."

I braced my back. "Why?"

With his free hand, he raked his fingers through his hair. "I didn't think anyone else would understand. How many people would believe I could be so `different?'" He glanced at the trophies. "And that isn't the word they'd use. It's kind, compared to what they'd say." Jordan laughed bitterly. "And what would you say, Amy?"

The weighted silence crushed me. *That I still love you.* I took a deep breath. "I don't know, Jordan."

* * *

I watched him climb the social ladder, eventually graduating law school and opening a practice in Oklahoma City, leaving me in Lawton, nearly two hours away. I drove to the city one day to go shopping and decided to cruise the parking lot of his firm. By coincidence, he was getting out of his car and spotted me. He walked over, and I rolled down the window.

"Well," he asked. "What do you think of my humble establishment?" He gestured toward the building.

Had I not seen his picture recently, I would hardly have recognized him. His dark navy suit looked so formal.

"It's great!" I said. "You've done well."

He nodded and stared at his office vacantly. Then he turned to me. "And you. How have you been, Amy?" His voice softened, the warmth of his tone curling around my name.

"Fine."

"Fine?" he quipped. "That's all you're going to say?" He shook his head reprovingly. "For that, you'll have to take an early lunch with me." He didn't wait for my reply, but hurried around the car and got in.

On the way to the restaurant we talked non stop, and it was only after we arrived, were seated, and had ordered that I realized how nothing we had said went beyond the aesthetics of our lives, the weather, our cars and our careers. The conversation had all the trappings of friendship but lacked the spontaneity, the raw emotion to bind it.

Nervously, I drank the red wine Jordan had ordered. At first the bitter taste exploded in my mouth. Then I grew accustomed to it and asked for a refill. I unfolded my napkin in my lap. "So how have you been?"

A soft smile lit his face. "Great. And you?"

"Me, too," I affirmed. "Have things changed any?" I braided my fingers together to halt the trembling.

He unfolded his napkin and his cheeks turned a light pink. "You mean have I changed, right?" I nodded hesitantly. "It's an easy word to say, Amy. Webster's doesn't define homosexual as a type of plague." I nodded and looked away. "Why did you come?"

Lifting the glass to my lips, I took a sip to wash down the godawful lump. I could feel him staring. "We never really spoke after breaking up." I glanced up, hoping my face didn't betray the pain inside. "I kept thinking you'd change your mind." I took another hasty swallow. "But you never did. I always thought I'd be beside you when you opened your practice." I stared at my empty glass and asked for another refill. "I wondered what your life might be like now."

The waiter returned with our orders and my wine, but I had lost my appetite. Instead of enjoying the food, I picked at it, nibbling, but the wine slid down my throat.

"Shouldn't you slow down?" Jordan frowned. "You still can't accept my choice, can you?"

I twisted the napkin, wondering how hard I had to pull before the fabric ripped. "You think I can't deal with who you've become. But that's not it." I took a deep breath.

"So what is it?"

"It never crossed my mind that you'd choose a road I couldn't go down. Remember how we talked about waiting until you finished law school before having a baby? We were going to call her Caitlyn Noel. Do you remember?"

The wine had gone to my head, and I knew my voice was too loud as other patrons abruptly stared. The waiter appeared and Jordan whispered in his ear. I felt my cheeks turning bright red. I had to get out of there.

Jordan excused himself for a moment and I slumped against the chair, feeling tears coming. I pressed my long nails deeply into my palms. A different pain to help forget. Jordan slipped behind me and gently pulled me from the chair. "Let's go somewhere a bit more private." I nodded, handing him the keys.

As he drove, I felt tired. "I shouldn't have ordered the wine, but you seemed so tense, like you needed something."

"You, Jordan," I mumbled. "You were all I ever needed." I opened my eyes to see him rake his fingers through his hair.

"Don't do this. Not now." He turned on the radio. He reached over and touched my face. "You're drunk, Amy."

I laughed, even my chest felt like it was going to explode. "Then I can say anything I want. I could ask you why." The breath caught in my throat and exited in a painful gasp. "But it doesn't matter, Jordan." I pushed his hand away savagely because I didn't want him to feel my heart seeping from my eyes. "Goddamn you!" I struck his arm. He didn't try to deflect the punches. "Are you happy now? Is there someone who gives you everything? Does he turn you on?" I screamed, but he kept looking at the road. His shoulders were rigid and he clenched the steering wheel. "I'm not drunk enough." I slumped against the seat.

"The hell you're not." That was the last thing I heard.

I woke in Jordan's bed, the soft, cotton comforter molded to my body. Jordan sat in a chair a few feet away. The formal jacket was gone, carefully draped across the chair. He had freed his tie from a knot, leaving it casually dangling from about his neck. The top shirt button was undone, and the long sleeves were rolled up. His once clean shaven face now seemed shadowy, hinting at a new, stubbly growth underneath. All but a strand of his thick, brown hair was brushed away from his face.

By a single lamp's light, our eyes met, but before I could search his, he looked away. "I'm sorry I hurt you." He looked at the floor and his eyebrows bunched together, as though he were thinking. "I never forgot about you, Amy. It's like in all the years, you were the one sacred thing in my life." He looked at me. "Because I knew you loved me. Without requirements or amendments." He rubbed his nose, and I thought I saw tears.

He walked to the bed and sat next to me. Taking my hand, he pressed it against his chest. "What I feel for you is in here, Amy. It's doesn't feed on physical attention." The neutral line of his mouth tugged downward into a painful frown. His face crumpled in pain. "God, don't think I don't love you, Amy. I'm just not in love with you."

Under my hand I could feel his heart hammering, and I pulled away. "This hurts too much, Jordan." I lay against the pillow. "I know I don't have a reason to hope, but that doesn't make giving up easier. You still live in me."

His eyes closed, as though he waited for the ceiling to fall. "I can't do this, Amy." He opened his eyes and stared at the ceiling. "My secretary saw us talking in the parking lot, and she asked me if we were going out. She said you were beautiful." His voice thickened.

I got up from the bed. "But not to you, Jordan. I've asked myself 10,000 times what went wrong, why it didn't work." He tried to grab my arm, but I pulled away. "God, you don't know what it's like to want someone so damn bad you could list the things you'd give away to have them." The color drained from his face and he looked like he was holding his breath. "You can't be human, not to hurt like this." I saw his shoulders slump. "How can it be that I love you so much that I don't know when to stop?" My voice sounded staccato from each rapid breath. *I won't cry. I won't let it out.*

"Amy."

"Don't say anything else. It won't change anything." I walked to the door, but he stepped in front of me and latched onto my arms.

"I never wanted to hurt you, and sometimes I wish that you hadn't loved me because it must be hell right now. But you're wrong. I am human, and I am hurting." He pulled me against his chest and held me there.

"Let me go," I screamed, struggling. His arms tightened, drawing me to him.

"Amy," he said softly. "For once don't fight. Just let it be. Let me hold you." I tried to swing at him, but he wouldn't let me.

I started sobbing and sinking into him. Jordan didn't ask me not to cry. He didn't ask himself not to either, but I think even with all the tears, we knew we could never reach salvation. Not like this. Not knowing love could be so unequal Not knowing whatever bound us together could also destroy us.

That night I drove away and tried to forget the beautiful Victorian house where he lived. I tried not to see imagined pictures of the two of us scattered throughout or which bedrooms would have been our children's. We would have no children. We would have no life together.

A month passed without Jordan. Then a few, but even so, I still felt him beside me as I read "To a Skylark" aloud. That was his favorite poem. And if I listened hard enough,

I heard his voice join mine, the warm tenor wrapping around me like a blanket. I thought of him often and wondered when I would see him again. That was the only thing I prayed for anymore. Just to rekindle a memory.

Then, six weeks ago, I sat on my porch swing, enjoying the spring breeze when his car pulled to the curb. Two years had passed. As he stepped out, he glanced at me, wearing a neutral expression. He stood as though waiting for me to make the first move. His eyes looked wide, almost nervous. I waved.

Once Jordan saw my hand, as well as the beginnings of a smile, he, too, grinned and walked toward the porch. As he started up the steps, I noticed his jeans and polo shirt, almost reminiscent of the senior I'd dated. He looked thinner. "Hello, Amy," he said quietly. "The house looks the same."

I nodded. "Yeah, and the swing still creaks."

He sat beside me. "I've missed you." He looked around and his gaze stopped at my face. His fingers curled around mine, softly, as though they would melt if I didn't want them there.

Needles of ice pricked me. I closed my fingers into fists and tried to ignore the fear. I wanted to believe Jordan had finally made it home, but I knew better. "How long are you here for?" I said the words slowly, not wanting an answer.

Jordan pushed the swing back and forth with his feet. "I don't know." He opened his mouth, but couldn't find the words he wanted. So he settled for, "I just don't know."

I let out a brittle laugh that sounded like a cough. God, how long had I waited. I stood and walked to the other end of the porch. My arms wrapped around my body tightly.

"Amy, I'm sick." He said it as one might say "The sky is blue."

Illness? I held my breath. *Please, God, don't let it be AIDS. I'll do anything for him, give anything, God. Please.* I thought about the things I would give for him, but my heart was already taken, and what use would a body be to God? He could take it as easily as he had given it, and I still wouldn't have Jordan.

I kept my back to him and pressed the pain deeper inside. No, tears. Not now. "It'll pass," I said closing my eyes.

"No," he replied. "It won't."

Why? *Why bring him back to me for this?* I mentally screamed. *How many times must I learn I can't have him?* I savagely brushed a stray hair out of my eyes. "I'm sorry," I managed in a hoarse voice. I made myself turn. I wasn't prepared for the single tear rolling down his face.

"I could never deserve your friendship,

let alone your love, but you gave them to me." He walked toward me and touched my face with his forefinger. "I just knew if there was anyone I needed to see, to be with, it was you." His gaze lingered on my face, waiting. His Adam's apple moved as he swallowed. "I don't have anywhere else to go. No one to stay with."

As I held my breath, I felt like my chest would explode. I didn't want to breathe, as though the simple exchange of oxygen would make this real. The air slipped out of my lungs and I inhaled. My knees wobbled slightly, but I braced them. I forced a smile through my tears. "Welcome home, Jordan."

For six weeks I lived only in the present. Jordan slept on my bed. I took the couch. And sometimes at night I'd slip into the room and stare at his face, liking the way it looked without lines to map the pain of where he'd been or where he was now. And for a second, I'd stand still, losing myself in him, in what might have been, in the way his chest rose and fell. I'd wrap my arms around my chest and the chills would still come. Tears would follow.

The days sometimes blurred together. The illness, the fevers, the pain. Yet, each night remained distinct. A new memory of him. And every evening, I'd take a long shower that left my skin pink from hot water. The rawness never went away.

But I never felt clean. Or whole.

It was the pneumonia which made me call 911. His temperature jacked up to 104 and I couldn't get it down. As they loaded him onto the gurney, I stared at the blue sheet which had swathed his body. I clutched the edge, thinking, *He won't be back. I should take it off.* And then I brought it to my chest and let my tears consecrate it. "Oh, God, please. Just one more day." My voice broke. "Just one," I whispered. And then I got into the ambulance with him.

By that night he couldn't get out of the hospital bed, and I had gotten pretty good at lists. And still I bargained. I learned to hate flowers. And my body despised me for sleeping on the pull-out bed or sitting in the waiting room for hours. My eyes forgot what daylight looked like. And I tried to trade the sun for an extension on his life.

I walked into his room and turned off some of the bright lights. I sat next to him and I felt him staring. He had grown thin, and once again I didn't really know him by appearance, but rather the way my heart pounded against my chest, as though fighting to strengthen him, to give him some part of me that might make him well. God, what good was love when it couldn't buy even one more night of laughter or pain or anything beyond this?

He slipped his hand into mine and said,

"I was waiting for you." His raspy voice dwindled to a whisper.

I put my other hand over his and patted it. "You knew I'd come." I took a deep breath, trying to make my chest into a wall. It might as well have been one because every breath hurt as though I slammed into something hard.

Jordan nodded slightly. Another wheezy breath. "Why? Why were you always there for me?" He spoke slowly, softly. "I failed you. I wasn't your husband, even though you wanted me." He blinked as though almost falling asleep, and I held my breath, wondering if he closed his eyes, would they open again. "Why did you stay?"

I looked at his hands, overcome by the miracle of holding them, feeling his fingers surrounding mine. "Because I loved you." My voice wavered, and my vision blurred. I blinked, trying to clear the haze. "And I still do."

I felt his hand touch my face and I pushed it against my cheek, trying to ignore the heat of his skin. I looked at him, at the thin line of his lips betraying a smile. "I've never met anyone who could believe like you, Amy. You had enough faith for us both." He squeezed my hand. "I'm so tired."

I closed my eyes and held his hand. I leaned over and rested on his chest. I listened to his heartbeat and felt mine stirring, rising toward him. Exhaustion came at me.

A shrill beeping jarred me awake. Nurses jostled me from the room as the doctor tried to revive him. *Save a place for me,* I thought, wondering if I glanced at the ceiling would I see his soul rising.

* * *

I shiver while walking through the empty parking lot. The night air is cold, but not as frigid as what lives in me. Maybe I do believe. Maybe now I understand. Maybe Purgatory is another name for earth, and whatever lies beyond is where Jordan waits for me.

Maria Rachel Hooley is the author of over twenty novels, including When Angels Cry, Sojourner, and New Life Incorporated. Her poetry has been published in over eighty national journals, including *Kimera*, *Green Hills Literary Lantern*, and *Slant*. Her first poetry chapbook, *A Different Song*, was published by Rose Rock Press in 1999. When she isn't writing, she teaches English to high school and college students. Hooley lives in Oklahoma with her husband and three children. Purgatory, a mainstream short story, placed second in the Oklahoma Writers Federation, Incorporated's 1998 writing competition.

Being Regular
K.A. Thompson

I spent $1.15 on a soda so small it could send a thirsty toddler into a major meltdown. And they call it a "tall," not "microscopic, two sips and you're done, small" as they probably should. The cup—and I just measured—is just a tad taller than my middle finger is long. And trust me, I have small hands.

Still, because I sit here in the café, taking up space, I felt compelled to buy the drink. It's not as if I don't really want it, I do; it's the idea of dropping over a dollar for less soda than I could get in a 25 cent can of WalMart's house brand (which, in my esteemed opinion, is pretty darned tasty.) I'm not the only one. There were seven or eight other people in here, doing what I'm doing— pretending to work or study—and all purchased the obligatory cheapest menu item to feel justified in taking up space.

Somehow I doubt the bookstore police (oh, yeah...the café is in a bookstore) are going to storm in and beat us all about the head and shoulders with wet sweat socks if we wander in and sit down without buying anything. It's the principle of the matter: you take up a business's space, you buy at least a small part of their product.

I do this a lot. I wrote at least half of a novel sitting in this café (but hey, not all in one day...), and have taken notice of the regulars here. Many seem to be students of the university down the road, in search of a quiet place to study and work on class assignments. I've often felt the impulse (but never acted on it) to point out that the McDonalds just across the street from the school, is usually just as quiet, and a whole lot cheaper.

I know that because I wrote part of a novel there, too.

Come to think of it, of the three novels I've written, most of them were penned in McD's, the café, the food courts of Travis AFB and Wright Patterson AFB, Burger King, and Taco Bell.

There's a pattern there

And it's evident: writing books contributes to weight gain.

But, the regulars.

Of all the regulars, the most visible is

Douggy. I know his name only because some of the employees greet him with the same infectious enthusiasm that the regulars on *Cheers* greeted Norm. They gleefully call out his name, and instantly have ready for him his favorite beverage along with a cookie or brownie. They watch for him; when someone notices Douggy in the parking lot, it's a race to the door to let him in, and accompany him to the café where his favorite table, or one close to it, is cleaned off, and where he is served.

Douggy is most visible because he arrives via the county bus-taxi service in a large and brightly painted motorized wheelchair, and because he is carefully fed his cookie or brownie by the blonde girl who works behind the counter, as they carry on a conversation only she can really understand.

People stare, and whisper, as people are wont to do. Most of the regulars smile and wave their fingers when Douggy arrives, acknowledging him as one of us. A person and not a sideshow.

The day I inadvertently sat at Douggy's table, engrossed in my own work (or perhaps a game of computer Scrabble; it's hard to remember, but with my work ethic...it was probably Scrabble), no one said anything, but as the door to the bookstore was held open, my internal voice piped up, and I casually moved to another table.

Confetti did not pour from some hidden spot in the ceiling. No one cheered or offered me a bright and shiny Mylar balloon for my consideration. My moving was expected; not required, but expected. Kind of like what anyone would do if they were perched upon Norm's *Cheers* stool. The courteous thing to do is move, without fanfare and without expectation.

There's another guy I see here quite often. He sits with his back to the window, holding a coffee cup between his hands, and he watches people in the café. Well, he stares. And he doesn't seem to care that people not only realize he's staring at them, but it makes them uncomfortable. I tend to think of him as "Creepy Guy" (not to be confused with the old man at the YMCA pool who stares at me while I swim. He's "Creepy Old Guy.")

I'm not sure I've ever seen Creepy Guy take a sip from the coffee cup he holds possessively between his hands. As far as I can tell, he just buys the thing to have a reason to sit there and stare.

There's an older couple (older than me, in any case, and these days I'm quite happy to find people older than me out and about) who are here almost every time I am. They each buy a coffee and a freakishly large cookie, then sit at a table for two, where they talk about their grandkids (perfect little angels, of course, even the one who whipped it out and peed on the fake tree at the mall food court), the trips they've taken (making me want to go see the World's Biggest Ball Of Twine, too), and their finances. That last one usually sparks a tense, teeth-clenched, under-the-breath argument about shoes she doesn't need, and tools he's too stupid to use correctly. As far as I can see, he hasn't yet cut a finger off, but she reminds him that he did sand a hole through one of the chairs that goes to her grandmother's antique dining set.

That shuts him up for a minute, and I'm pretty sure she's headed to the mall and every store that sells spiffy new shoes. Often—though not as often as I see other people—there's this young woman (25 or thereabouts) who brings her young son; most of the time she has just bought him a new book, and he sits at the table, pretending he can read. His face is unusually serious for a three year old, but it's a seriousness borne of determination: he will read the entire text of *If You Give a Mouse a Cookie* before they leave. When he's done, he slams the book closed and proclaims, "That's just not right."

I'm not sure what's not right. Mice do like cookies; I've seen one try to carry off an entire Oreo. And I'd think that if you did give a mouse a cookie, or a part thereof, you'd be obligated to follow through.

There's usually an odd assortment of FrankenWalkers, kids just learning to master their own feet, and quite often they're fascinated by what must be extremely new shoes. They walk with their heads down, staring at the contraptions Velcroed in place; I now understand this, having recently acquired a spiffy new pair of red, white, and blue Converse Chuck Taylor's. Yes, for the first day or so, I frequently watched my feet, enthralled by the canvas pseudo-flags sticking out from the bottom of my jeans.

Okay. Yes. I'm 42 years old. I bought shoes better suited to a 16 year old. But they're spiffy. They're Chucks. And they match my brand new red, white, and blue leather flag jacket.

It's not a midlife crisis thing. Not even accounting for the fact that last year I bought a shiny red convertible. Nope.

Do I wonder what the other regulars think about the middle aged housewife who sits there with a notebook or sometimes a laptop computer, scribbling or tapping away, dressed like a backwards teenager?

Sometimes. But I'm fairly sure I'm not as interesting to them as they are to me. At least not on the days I'm not talking to myself.

Once in a while, kids (especially those who are there often) will walk up and ask what I'm doing (and as tempted as it is, I've never answered "writing porn; go ask Mommy what that is.") and start a conversation to the horror of their parents—parents who were paying such close attention that they failed to notice when their precious offspring wandered away.

Most of them are attracted by my jacket; that's my assumption, spurred on by a two year old who pointed at me and squealed "Fag!"

That's toddler-speak for "flag."

Right?

The thing about the regulars: while we acknowledge each other, we do not speak to each other. It's silent courtesy; we know we're not there to socialize for the most part. Some of us are there to write the next Great American Novel, some are there to scratch out the Perfect Term Paper, some to unwind, to reconnect with the person on the other side of the same table, but we're not there to make friends. Any details we know about one another are discovered only through bits and pieces of overheard conversations.

Until today.

Douggy has not been seen in the café in over a week. His absence has been noticed, definitely, but people miss days here and there. Being at the café from 1-3 p.m. is not a requirement, and there is Real Life out there. So the first few days of Douggy's absences were noted, but not with concern.

But today Creepy Guy put his cup down on the table, and asked of no one in particular, "Where's Douggy?"

Everyone looked up from what they were doing and glanced at Douggy's vacant table. Not only was Douggy not there, but the blonde who always greeted him with an explosive smile and cookies, who patiently fed him and wiped his chin of crumbs and dribbles, always with the utmost care and respect, was also absent.

So today we talked, comparing mental notes. "When did you last see him?" "How was he? Looking tired? Happy? What?" "What about the girl? Anywhere around so we can ask her?"

We moved from our respective spots and sat together, wondering out loud where the kid with the bright grin and killer wheels was. As far as we could figure out, no one had seen him in at least a week. Neither had we seen the blonde girl.

Our loud conversation caught the ear of the other girl working behind the café counter; she set aside her towel and came over to us, pulling over a chair from another table.

The blonde is Douggy's sister.

And Douggy, who evidently refused to allow his disability to get the better of him, bravely driving his brightly painted wheelchair on even the busiest of streets, entered a crosswalk at precisely the moment the driver of a minivan chose to answer her cell phone.

She took her eyes off the road just long enough to miss the fact that the kid in the wheelchair had rolled off the sidewalk. Just long enough for her to plow into him at full speed. At 45 miles an hour.

Douggy never had a chance.

The blanketing silence was an uncomfortable pause of concern; in a movie it would have exploded like a spent bubble, anger demanding retribution, the driver of the minivan's head on a platter.

Reality is rarely captured on film.

One by one we retreated to our former tables. And then one by one people left. Students went to their classes. The older couple headed out, and as he shoved his empty cup into the trash can he commented on the sale at shoe store just down the street. The café girl went back to work, cleaning the counter.

I looked at my too-expensive toddler soda, wondering what I should think. What I should feel. I did not know Douggy, not in the least. I do not know what caused him to live out his life in a motorized wheelchair, or even how long he had been in it. I never guessed that the blonde was his sister.

I never thought to ask.

I never presumed to strike up a conversation with Douggy or his sister. Or anyone else.

I'm here to work.

I come in here and pay too much money for too little drink, so I can work.

Creepy Guy pushed himself up with a loud sigh, crumpling the foam coffee cup in his hand. He paused before heading for the door, and looked at me. Not in my general direction, but at me, he looked into my eyes.

"I'll see ya around," he said. "Take care."

K.A. Thompson is the author of eight books, which include the *Charybdis* series: *Charybdis*, *As Simple as That*, *Finding Father Rabbit*, and *The King and Queen of Perfect Normal.*

America,
Land of Mysteries
Ricky Sides

Polymer found in unlikely location.

Please bear with me as I lay out the background information necessary for you to understand what I am about to relate. I shall try to be as succinct as possible.

In the mid 1980s I underwent a survival training regimen with a veteran of the US armed forces. A portion of this training dealt with fashioning an emergency shelter in the forest should the need arise. The two of us approached a mutual friend seeking permission to utilize his property for this training as he had a parcel of land ideally suited for our intended purpose.

The section that we selected for this

training was a thinly wooded hillside. My trainer wanted me to learn how to fashion a small man-made cave shelter. The most efficient and effective design burrows into a hillside at a slight upward angle so that any precipitation will drain off back down the hillside and not into the entrance, thus creating a soggy mess inside the cave. This is effective because as you burrow inside the hillside the ground above your tunnel entrance rapidly thickens, thus providing insulation against the bitter cold of winter with a minimum of labor on your part. Achieving the same results on flatland requires considerably more labor and drainage becomes a much more critical issue.

Such a one- or two-man shelter can be completed in just a few hours unless you have the misfortune to encounter a rather large rock or small boulder. Unfortunately at two or three feet inside the hillside that is precisely what happened to us. We encountered a smallish boulder. We hoped that this was just a finger of limestone rock that we could rapidly break through and continue with the project. A few minutes of hammering at this limestone rock and I had penetrated its surface a few inches.

It was at this point that I noted a splash of color embedded in the rock surface that I had just exposed. I stopped working and leaned in closer for a better look at the red object I had just exposed. Yet only the small-est fragment of the item was visible. I blew the dust away and then called my trainer's attention to the item. We consulted for a moment and decided that it might be inter-esting to preserve the item intact.

Taking a brick hammer, I used the pick end and scribed a rough square roughly four inches by four inches with the splash of red being in the center. I then placed the point of the pick against one edge that I had just scribed and my trainer gently tapped my brick hammer with his own. Soon we had three edges of this scribed deeply and be-gan to work on the fourth. The second tap of my partner's hammer caused the center section of the scribed area to break and fall away.

I picked up this section and turned it over to examine the back side. There I found a smallish wafer of red material embedded in the limestone rock. We carefully chipped away at the rock until it broke and the wa-fer came free. I noted that a portion of the rock I held in my hand bore a partial im-pression of the red wafer. You could clearly see where half of it had rested for god knows how long inside that limestone boulder bur-ied two or three feet inside the hillside.

I slipped the wafer and that piece of rock inside a pocket to keep because it was proof that the wafer had indeed been buried inside the rock. My trainer congratulated me on the find which he agreed was quite interesting.

Later that day I spoke to the landowner and asked his permission to keep the item as a curiosity piece. Being a good friend, he agreed to let me keep it, though by rights it belonged to him as it was found on his property.

For years I kept the piece of rock which bore the partial impression and the wafer in a plastic bag and showed it to friends as a conversation piece. One day I was showing this item to a friend who became intently interested in the wafer which was one-inch long by one-half-inch wide by one-eighth-inch thick. These measurements are accurate. This friend offered to have the item analyzed by a friend of his who worked for a lab.

I agreed reluctantly with the stipulations that I did not want the item destroyed and I wanted it back. It took a few weeks to get the results but one day at work my friend returned my items and handed me a short note detailing the results of the analysis. The note was handwritten by the technician who had performed the test.

That was so long ago that I cannot remember the exact wording of the tech's note but here is the gist of the man's analysis: The wafer was composed of a polymer similar to that of which bowling balls are composed. The tech had inquired of my friend as to where the sample had originated because he had also seen the rock with the impression of the wafer embedded in its surface. My friend had not revealed the location because I had stressed that I wanted my landowner friend's privacy protected and was concerned that his privacy would be encroached upon by the curious should the location become known. He had however revealed the rest of the details. The tech had informed him that this was indeed a mystery as polymers had not existed long enough for the wafer to end up where it had eventually been located.

This piqued my curiosity and I researched polymers. The first polymers were invented in the 1800s. Yet this sample had been found below ground embedded inside a limestone rock. This led me to research the formation of limestone rock. I won't bore you with all of the details. Suffice it to say that it takes hundreds and hundreds if not thousands of years longer than polymers have existed for limestone rock to form.

A few years after this another friend decided to purchase the property where this item had been unearthed when the original landowner had put it up for sale. I gave the items and the note from the technician to this man. I felt a moral obligation to make the offer as he was now owner of the property and I hadn't even looked at the items in years. This man later went through a divorce and the items were lost in the chaos that followed. He also sold the parcel of land on which the items had been unearthed. I have no idea who owns it now.

I now deeply regret my decision to part with those items, but you live and learn.

Mystery lightning bug display.

In the mid 1980s my survival trainer and I were in a remote area about 16 miles from the city where I live. The property was at one time a fish hatchery. Once the old fish hatchery had been closed it was opened to the public for recreational purposes. We used the fish hatchery for camping and training purposes.

Adjacent to the fish hatchery was a rectangular-shaped fenced-in pasture. The pasture is surrounded on three sides by woods. It is about the width of two football fields but as long as several with a thin ribbon of forest separating one side from a river which loops around the entire fish hatchery.

One night my trainer and I were on a night patrol, the purpose of which was to train me in the art of traveling woodlands at night with no light source. We came to the fenced-in pasture and stared in amazement at the display of the lightning bugs located over the pasture.

There must have been hundreds of thousands if not millions of the insects present over that pasture and they were synchronized. The lightning bugs at the end of the pasture nearest us would flash on and off and then the ones a bit further out into the pasture did the same. This flashing further and further away continued until it disappeared at the furthest range of our vision and then the cycle began again. For some ten minutes we stood observing this phenomenon and then we eventually moved away to return to base camp.

If you have ever seen airport runway lights you can envision what we saw. Just cover an huge field with sets of those lights in your mind and synchronize them all.

I should point out that we often returned to that area but never again did we witness this strange phenomenon. I sincerely wish that we'd had a video camera with us, but in those days such cameras were terribly expensive and massively bulky so of course we did not own one and wouldn't have risked it in that environment on a pitch black night even if one of us had owned one.

That fish hatchery was closed to the public a few years ago and is no longer available for public recreation.

Mystery Harmony heard with electronic listening device.

There is one more mystery that my survival training partner and I encountered in the mid 1980s in the old fish hatchery that I will relate.

Electronic listening devices can be utilized in some situations as a means to detect danger near you in hostile territory. Such devices had been created and were being marketed to the public. Actually the unit that we were using was little more than a toy. It consisted of a small parabolic dish with a pistol grip and a headset plugged into it with basic volume controls on the handheld unit. The unit was by no means as powerful as those used by law enforcement, yet for training purposes it was a useful tool.

We'd been training with the unit extensively that day and as dusk began to settle in we noted that the batteries had been pretty severely drained. As we wanted to train with the unit at night when a human's sense of hearing is more critical I changed out the batteries in the unit and then held it up and pointed it in the direction in which I was gazing. As it so happens I was noting the position of the setting sun and speculating in my mind as to whether or not we would see the odd lightning bug synchroni-zation again. We had set up our base camp near that pasture in the hopes of witness-ing a repetition of that event, though it had been some weeks since we had observed the phenomenon.

I turned on the power and adjusted the volume as the last glimpses of the sun dis-appeared behind the trees. The bionic ear crackled static in my ears as I slowly tracked it in the direction in which I was gazing and then suddenly the static disappeared and was replaced with a very unusual sound. I must confess that I have never been able to explain what I heard properly, but never-theless I will attempt to do so to the best of my ability.

I heard what sounded like a multitude of voices singing in harmony. But there were not really words being sung. It was like they were holding notes with their voices for an impossibly long time and then changing to another note on the scale. Also it should be noted that I've had considerable musical training both in school and in my personal life. It is my opinion that the notes we heard were beyond the capability of the human voice. Most certainly no human can hold a note for the duration that we observed. There were no accompanying musical instruments.

The phenomenon was not something that we could detect without the listening device. My facial expression informed my training partner that I was intently listening to something and he queried me as to what so captivated my attention. I mutely removed the headset and handed it to him carefully holding the small parabolic dish in the direction in which I had located the strange sound. He equipped the headset and listened just as intently as I had to the strange sounds emanating from the listening device. With no feedback from the headset I soon lost the sound and my partner took the dish and found it immediately.

My partner and I took turns listening for about 15 minutes and then we lost the sound for the night. In a moment of mental clarity, which I confess is sort of rare for me, I noted that the sound had begun as the sun disappeared from view, thus the two events might be connected. My partner and I vowed to try to catch that sound again the next time we were there. We managed to do so upon one other occasion. That occurrence duration was approximately the same in all aspects. Shortly after this second experience the device was broken in a training accident. We did not replace the unit as it had served its purpose and they were not exactly cheap.

Last year I learned about a phenomenon called Angelic voices. There are some claims that people have recorded the sounds of Angels singing. These voices are not audible to the human ear but electronic recording devices can pick them up and the playback reveals them. This intrigued me as the voices thus recorded also hit notes which seem to be beyond human capacity in both duration and vocal range. I've heard samples of these so-called Angelic voices. The ones singing harmony do indeed sound similar to what my training partner and I heard in the old fish hatchery though neither of us ever heard any discernible words in our two experiences.

I should also note that upon the second occasion that we detected the sounds, a visitor arrived at our camp while the phenomenon was occurring. He also heard the sounds through the headset.

Ricky Sides was born in Florence, Alabama, in May of 1958. The author's writing experience includes the science fiction, action adventure book The Birth of the Peacekeepers and the other books in the series. The author also wrote the fantasy, action adventure Brimstone and the Companions of Althea series which is a nine novel set, based on the online game t4c (the fourth coming) and was written by Ricky Sides under the pen name Raistlin and edited and collaborated on by a wonderful lady from Louisiana under the pen name Kittie Justice. The author also wrote a book on women's self-defense named The Ultimate in Women's Self-Defense.

rsides22219@charter.net
http://www.sonofartherk.com

Dime a Dip
Edward Cliffe Patterson

*For my grandmother Margaret Elizabeth Cliffe
(1904-1987)*

1

"The next prospect's a pain in the ass,"
Mary said, twisting the rear view mirror, and
then puckering her lips to reapply some ruby
gloss. "A real pain in the ass. Buckle up."

I didn't know Mary well. She acted casually around me, although I was the boss.
However, I was new on the scene; new to
Orange County — new to California. She was
the sales rep, and I the observer. Still, she
made me feel like a kid driven to school by
his mother.

"A pain?" I asked. "How so?"

"They're all pains. Even those who buy.
Although they're prospects, they're dull

pains. When they're customers, they're got-you-by-the-titties pains."

"Or the balls."

"Balls. Titties. They control it all. Buckle up."

I hated sales calls, especially with a smart-ass, know-it-all rep who was taking advantage of my substitute-boss status. In from headquarters, I was babysitting for the Orange County office, while the appointed sales manager recuperated from a motorcycle accident.

Lucky man, I thought. *No sales calls for him.*

Mary sped away, babbling about her perfect sales technique, obviously an attempt to score points. I didn't hear a word of it. It was all crap. People bought what they wanted when they wanted. No amount of coaxing from some bimbo with ruby gloss lips mattered. If you were in the right spot at the right moment, you got the sale. Be on the spot enough and you would be honored as *Sales Person of the Month*, earning enough commissions for that extra scoop of pistachio at the local Dairy Queen.

"It's all in the timing," Mary said. "I can tell when they're ripe for the signing. Pen in their hand, I know. Gets the contract every time. Are you listening?"

I wasn't. I was watching a vast expanse of farmland from the open window. A warm breeze folded its new-mown aroma over my nose and . . . I remembered.

"Strawberries," Mary said.

"Excuse me?"

"The strawberries are up and the pickers are in. Migrant workers. They drift in about this time of year to pick the strawberries."

My eyes refocused. In the fields, dozens of migrants bent their backs over the crop, filling baskets with red, merry berries. Women scooped them up, while men hoisted the heavy loads into trucks. Children crawled about the rows for the loose stuff, like gamers playing marbles in the dust.

"Are you okay?" Mary asked.

I just stared, panning over those fields — sighing. I remembered.

2

"Fill 'er up," he said. "Marge, look at the price of gas. Only twenty-two cents a gallon."

"Well, that's Georgia," Marge said, sitting beside him in their 1954 green Nash Rambler and listening to Patty Page sing the *Tennessee Waltz* on the radio. "Oh, I love this song, Eddie."

"D'yall say fill 'er?" the attendant asked.

"That's fine. Fill 'er up. Yer have a terlet here? A place to pee?"

"Yessir. 'Tsright over there."

"Marge, do you gotta go?"

"No, Eddie. I'm fine."

Eddie left Marge tapping to her radio waltz. She lighted a cigarette and looked around.

Attracted by the sign for cheap gas, they had pulled off the main highway into a linden grove. Sultry Georgia felt unending — dusty roads and dull farmland. At least, under the lindens, a cool breeze sighed.

"Do yer want a stretch?" the attendant said as he pumped. "We hev a Coca-Cola cooler."

"No, I'm fine," Marge said, fanning herself with the latest issue of *Life*.

Marge relaxed to the music, puffing away, her auburn hair kept neatly pinned beneath a pink and gold silk scarf. She peered over her sunglasses at the surrounding piles of garage debris — old cars, wheels and hubcaps. Then, something caught her eye. Sitting on the running board of a rusty maroon truck, a barefoot child sat smoking a pipe. He couldn't have been more than five. Their eyes met, the boy smiling, shading his eyes after seeing her. His feet were caked with good, red Georgia clay. He wore rags.

"Excuse me," Marge said to the attendant. "That boy over there? Is he yours?"

"No. No m'am. None of them people are fit for company."

"Them people?"

"Migrant workers," he said, spitting some tobacky. "He's a migrant brat. Pay him no heed. His folk are sleepin' down by the crick. If he's a bother to yer m'am, I'll shoo 'em 'way."

"No, no. He's fine. He's just so . . ."

"So po'."

"Well, yes. And he has no shoes. His feet are torn up."

"It's to be 'spected when you toil on the ground fer yer livin'."

"Pretty clean terlet," Eddie said, returning. He paid the attendant, got in and revved the Nash. "Anything wrong, Marge?"

"No, nothing. Just, that boy over there. He looks so . . . forlorn. Migrant worker, you know. Cast off. Unwanted."

Marge drifted back to her childhood, cast off and unwanted, from aunts to grandfather to half sister — a touch and go existence that always loomed at her shoulder despite the security she now enjoyed. She signaled to the boy, who hopped off the running board.

"Don't encourage him," Eddie said. "We got to make time. We're doin' good so far on this route. Marge, don't encourage him."

"Hush, Eddie. How could a dime hurt?"

The boy looked up at his dirty-faced reflection in Marge's sunglasses. She stretched down and gave the boy a dime — a whole ten cents, almost half the price of a gallon of gas.

"For ice cream," she said. "I wish I could

buy you shoes, but only ice cream today."

The boy took the coin and wept.

"Eddie, let's go quick, before my heart breaks."

3

The Prospect Park Baptist Church stood on the corner of Avenue C and 3rd Street in Brooklyn, having been moved there years before from downtown to the wilds of Flatbush. A small church, formerly a chapel, it now stood on an ample lawn in a quiet residential neighborhood. Among the church's many events, the Junior Women, a ladies auxiliary, met once monthly to discuss and schedule their charitable activities.

"The floor recognizes Marge Cliffe," Madam President said. "Marge has a new idea for a fundraiser."

Two dozen heads turned as Marge stood and took the floor. Never a great public speaker, Marge usually shunned the spotlight. However, she felt compelled by this idea, perfect for the next charitable activity.

"Thank you, Anna," she said, looking about nervously. "As you know, Eddie and me just came back off a drive from Florida. I hope you got your postcards." She saw that many had. "We really enjoyed ourselves. It was a grand trip. Long, but grand — most of it through some very poor areas. Now, we were in this place called Conovertown, in Georgia; and while we were getting gas, I met a little migrant worker boy. He was so down on his luck. I just thought we might be able to send some money from our next fundraiser to help these children. I mean, they didn't even have shoes."

Mrs. Van Gelderfeder raised her pudgy hand.

"Yes, Hettie," Madam President said.

"There're lots of children without shoes, Marge," Hettie said, taking the floor. "My own neighbor's kids walk around barefooted all the time. Now I feel sorry for these tykes, but their parents have chosen a very difficult way to earn a living. Nomads in the fields. I think we should keep our money closer to home."

She sat. The women muttered softly — consensually.

"I see what you mean," Marge stammered. "But did you know that migrant workers are not just Southern drifters. They work the farms in Long Island." The ladies, surprised, whispered. "I have many facts about the migrant workers here in my papers. I sent away. It's interesting. Sad, but interesting. But to the point, this has nothing to do with what they do. It's about the children. Hettie, have you ever gone barefooted because your parents couldn't afford to keep you in shoes?"

Hettie sat up in her chair.

"Marge," Madam President said. "We all care about the children. Whenever we can bring relief to those tender lambs, we try. Just like Our Lord." Reverent silence. "Still, we should never ignore an opportunity to do the Lord's work. Just what did you have in mind, Marge?"

"Just a dinner," Marge said. "A simple dinner. Spaghetti, with donated sauce — home made. The good kind. We can all make sauce, can't we? My daughter'll help. The more we donate, the lower the expense, and the more money we can send for the children. I found an association that'll take the money and assured that goes strictly to help the migrant children."

Madame President folded her hands, slowly radiating a smile.

"All those in favor of a Spaghetti dinner to help the migrant worker children, say *aye*."

4

As the *ayes* had it, the great spaghetti event unfolded in the year of Our Lord 1956 with high expectations and excitement. Donated cakes, pounds of meat, simmered sauce and box after box of spaghetti mustered into the little church. On the lawn, games for the children and ice cream. Above it all, a diminutive Marge buzzed between tables and booths, supervising every detail.

"A dime a dip?" Mr. Forster-Brookings said. He was a tower of piety and strength in the church. "A bit steep for a ladle full of sauce, Marge, don't you think?"

"But you get the spaghetti for free, John," she answered. "Remember, a meat-ball is only a nickel. But you get no bread with one meatball."

"Four meatballs and two dips," John crowed. "How much for a sprinkle of cheese?"

"Free," Marge said. "Unless you want to donate a little something extra. Then I'll throw in a nice green side salad."

"Amazing," Anna said. "Everyone's having a wonderful time. It's a great event, Marge; and the last time I checked, the till was at a whopping . . ."

"$500," Marge said. She smiled, an inward radiation blossoming to her cheeks. "If I get to $600, I'll be happy. Lots of shoes for $600. Next year . . ."

"Next year?"

"Why, of course, unless you want to do it sooner? Next year, we'll add arts and crafts."

5

"Next year," Marge said, "you must assure that the Dime a Dip continues. I wish I could get up and run it from South Jersey, but it's impossible. Promise me."

"I don't see how we can stop it after thirty years," Anna said. "What's in the till today?"

"$8,000. Lots of . . ."

"Lots of shoes for $8,000. Bless you dear."

Marge beamed. She went into the kitchen and lit up, her slight gray form reflected in the stainless steel. Her auburn hair, long since honey blond by choice, neatly peeked out from beneath her scarf. She looked through the service window at the busy ladies and satisfied customers, taking their dime a dip, donating much more at checkout. Marge smiled. Something caught her eye. A man, in business attire, quite out of place for a spaghetti dinner, spoke with Anna. Anna pointed toward the kitchen door. The man approached Marge's restful inner sanctum.

"Mrs. Cliffe?" asked the man coming through the door.

"Yes, can I help you?"

"Can you help me?" he said. "That's the strangest question I thought would ever come from you. Can you help me?"

"I'm sorry. Do I know you?"

"I'm Kyle Andersen from the Georgia Migrant Workers Board."

"Oh, heavens," she said. "I've been sending a check to your organization for thirty years now. This is the first time anyone has come up to inspect. We run a clean shop here. Everything's donated and we make no profit."

"No, no, Mrs. Cliffe."

"Call me Marge. Cigarette?"

"No. I don't smoke anymore."

"Bad habit. I'll give it up someday."

"I'm here in a private capacity. I wanted to meet the woman who has raised over $200,000 for the migrant children. I wanted to meet her and thank her personally. Meet her again, at least."

"Again?"

"Yes, again. We met some years back."

"At the fundraiser? I don't remember you. Sorry. Has it been $200,000? Time goes so fast. Me and my husband, Eddie, just bought a house down in South Jersey. We're retiring there. I don't know how I can give all this up. But I believe it must be done. The ladies will run it again next year. I'm sure it will go on forever, if they can help it."

"Your efforts on our behalf have been tireless and faithful, Marge," he said, kissing her on the forehead. Flustered, she giggled. Kyle smiled broadly and reached into his pocket holding high a dime.

"That will buy you a dip," she said.

"A scoop," he said. "This dime was meant for a scoop."

"A scoop?"

"Yes, a scoop. This dime was given to me by a very kind lady years ago, who told me it was for ice cream."

Marge clutched the stainless steel sink as Kyle pressed the dime into her hand, retreating quickly back into her memory.

6

"Are you okay?" Mary asked. "We're almost there. Are you crying?"

I turned to her, the tears streaming down my face.

"It's the sun. That's all."

"Here, wipe them. I heard about your grandmother. I'm sorry. It takes time, you know."

"I know. Thanks."

I wiped my face quickly, and then quietly returned my gaze out the window. Mary had finally shut up. I thought to tell her about the great woman whose small contribution our generation would probably ignore, even in the footnotes. But such information is unworthy of the selfish. I kept it a secret as we crossed those California fields — the endless fields of strawberries, with their picking children — children in shoes now.

Never the End for those who Care

Edward C. Patterson has been writing novels, short fiction, poetry and drama his entire life, always seeking the emotional core of any story he tells. With his eighth novel, The Jade Owl, he combines an imaginative touch with his life-long devotion to China and its history. He has earned an MA in Chinese History from Brooklyn College with further postgraduate work at Columbia University. A native of Brooklyn, NY, he has spent four decades as a soldier in the corporate world gaining insight into the human condition. He won the 2000 New Jersey Minority Achievement Award for his work in corporate diversity. Blending world travel experiences with a passion for storytelling, his adventures continue as he works to permeate his readers' souls from an indelible wellspring.

Published Novels by Edward C. Patterson include *No Irish Need Apply, Bobby's Trace, Cutting the Cheese, Surviving an American Gulag, Turning Idolater, Look Away Silence, The Jade Owl* (Jade Owl Legacy Series Book I), *The Third Peregrination* (Jade Owl Legacy Series Book II), *The Dragon's Pool* (Jade Owl Legacy Series Book III), and *Southern Swallow Series* (Book I – *The Academician*). *Coming soon:* Southern Swallow Series (Book II – *The Nan Tu*; Book III – *Swan Cloud*; Book IV – *The House of Green Waters*), *Belmundus, The Road to Grafenwöhr,* and *Green Folly*. Look also for *The People's Treasure* (Jade Owl Legacy Series Book IV) and *In the Shadow of Her Hem* (Jade Owl Legacy Series Book V).

Poetry books available are *The Closet Clandestine: a queer steps out and Come, Wewoka & Diary of Medicine Flower*. Also *Are You Still Submitting Your Work to a Traditional Publisher?*

The author can be found online at http://www.dancaster.com

Uncle Aleister
Randolph Lalonde

It came at night. A punishment for being awake after he ought to be fast asleep. He couldn't help it. Sometimes Barney's bedroom door creaked closed and his eyes popped open. It left him with the painted poppet he'd been given last year for his sixth birthday, that cheery thing that leered in the dark of the evening from his rickety hand-me-down dresser.

As if the worry of German bombings wasn't enough, there was something lurking in the shadows. It paid no mind to the faint sound of the BBC Radio murmuring and crackling in the next room. The shapeless beast listened to the floor boards as closely as Barney did while his uncle paced to and fro in the front room down the hall.

The smell of Uncle Aleister's pipe, smouldering vanilla tobacco, faintly wafted in under the door. Still the creature paid no mind to the ample evidence of adults nearby as he waited for Barney to make his move.

Was the creature in the closet this time? Its door was open just a crack, and beyond that portal was darkness, a perfect onyx shadow for it to hide in. It could be under the bed, eagerly waiting for little feet to sneak out from under the covers and reach for the floor. Quick claws and great jaws could be waiting just beneath his mattress to snatch at his heels and drag him into the beast's dark domain.

Perhaps he had it all wrong. Perhaps the creature was hanging outside his window, gripping the sill and watching the few pedestrians who braved the shady alleyway. It was just waiting for him to hide under the covers or drift off to sleep, then he'd be a nice midnight snack for the shadow monster.

Barney's heart beat a tattoo against his chest, his mouth was dry, and the covers felt heavy. He glanced to the cheerfully painted, leering poppet sitting on his dresser. It wouldn't be any help. Even if it knew where the beast hid, the bloody thing would be nothing more than mute witness.

The window slammed shut of its own accord, catching the curtains in its wooden maw. "It's here!" Barney shrieked with fright, sitting up like a shot and frantically searching the room with his wide eyes.

Long seconds passed in the darkness. Footsteps outside warned of Uncle's impending arrival and the door finally opened. The warm half-light of the hall laid a safe path across the bed and in came tall, aged Uncle Aleister. He strode directly to the edge of the bed, glass of water in one hand, the other pressed into the pocket of his old wool jacket. "What's this then?" he asked, his baritone voice accompanied with a slight wet rasp.

"The window, something's at the window!" Barney managed, pointing at the offending portal.

Uncle Aleister put the glass of water down on the bedside table and shuffled over. "Seems he's got more of an appetite for your mother's curtains than little boys," he chuckled, carefully lifting the old wooden window and tugging the curtains free.

Barney scanned the dimly lit room, looking for any trace of the beast. It always shrank away when his parents, relations or sitters came into the room. Where it went, he could never discern. His survey complete, Barney looked back to his Uncle who was just finishing jamming the window open with a piece of kindling.

"That should keep it up good and proper, no more bumps in the night," he nodded satisfactorily. His aged uncle fixed him with a look then. He was by far his favourite uncle, and though his cough kept him from playing, he told the most wondrous stories.

"But that's not what's got you up at this late hour, is it?"

Barney felt his face flush. He was too old to be afraid of the dark, his father had told him so time and time again. "Just the window Uncle," he muttered lamely.

Aleister ignored him, looking around the room instead. "Is it this dreadful thing? He's got to have a devil's grin at night." Two strides took him to the dresser where he snatched the cheery poppet and stuffed it into the top drawer. "Let's see you get out of that," he uttered triumphantly. A mild, wet cough wracked him for a moment before he looked to Barney. He covered his mouth with a kerchief briefly and shook his head as he recovered. "That's not it, is it boy?"

"No," Barney said with a sigh, hanging his head.

Uncle Aleister crossed the room and sat on the bed. "I know precisely what has you up. It's a bogeyman," he whispered conspiratorially. "Some of us can see them, even at my age, and I can tell as plain as the nose on my face one's been this way. Should've seen it before, shame on me."

Barney gripped the hems of his blankets, his eyes widened fear.

"Not to worry. I have just the thing." He pulled a small tin medal on a thin iron chain from his pocket. A face had been etched into it, but years of wear had worn parts of it away. "You didn't think I grew to this ripe old age without having a trick to repel the bogey, did you?"

"What is it?"

"It's an old hope medal. Now you put this 'round your neck and check all your corners. You'll find he's shrunk away."

"What will you use if you give me your medal?"

"No worries, I've made up with the old beastie."

"The bogeyman is your friend?"

Uncle Aleister nodded. "We've an under-standing, he and I. The beast knows I'm the master, no question, so I won't be needing a charm. Time for you to have a turn."

Barney let Uncle Aleister put the medal around his neck and peered at the medal closely. It was old, probably as old as the man who'd given it to him.

"Now check all his hiding places."

"Can you look?"

"Doesn't work if I do it. You've got to show him you've got the medal, then he'll leave you alone. So up, out of bed with you. Check the dark places as quick as a hare."

Barney had nothing to lose. There was a broad shaft of light across the room, his uncle was at his side and he had his new medal. Even with everything on his side he made haste as he hopped out of bed. He checked beneath the mattress to discover only a toy wooden aeroplane he'd forgotten, under the dresser and finally, the closet.

His uncle pointed. "Don't forget to check behind the door, lad."

Fortified by the first-hand evidence of the beast's absence, Barney rushed to the door and checked the shadow between it and the wall.

"Now back to bed. He's seen you with the medal so you just keep it at your bed-side and he'll be gone for good."

Barney took it off and handed it to his Uncle, who deposited it on the side table.

"He knows you mean business now, and to sod off and be some other boy's pest," the old gentleman reassured.

Uncle Aleister waited for him to settle under the covers and tucked him in tightly. "He'll be back, he always comes back," Barney mumbled.

"Perhaps, but you be sure and tell him who's boss. Bogeymen don't quarrel with boys who are brave enough to check their own closets, medal or not."

"Thank you Uncle," Barney said as Aleister kissed him on the forehead.

Even though he was so well tucked-in and comfortable, he couldn't resist taking the medal from the bedside table and put-ting it on. He drifted off as he turned it over in his hands, watching how the light of the street lamp outside reflected on it.

Two Weeks Later

Barney could be a bit of a handful after a visit from his Uncle Aleister. It was the same thing every time. The old bugger would visit, fill the child's head with stories and then leave London entirely, satisfied that he'd spent enough time spoiling his grandnephew. "Not like he's lacking for imagination, that one. Lad's got a head stuck in the clouds," Emily muttered to herself as she worked her embroidery. She had taken up residence while Barney's parents were in the country. The letter she'd received in the post before Aleister left explained that they would be further delayed, and she would find household funds in a tin tucked into the corner beside the coal chute.

The announcer on the radio was speaking about the events in the House of Commons that day. The Foreign Secretary had caused a stir, denouncing the Germans for executing Jews. She listened quietly, keeping her count of loops and stitches. She had difficulty believing it was as bad as they said.

A clatter down the hall interrupted her head shaking and loop counting. "What's that foolish lad up to?" she murmured to herself.

Barney's bedroom door opened. The drowsy boy rubbed the sleep out of his eye as he came walking down the hall. "Can I have some water?" he whined.

"You go on back to bed, I'll bring it to you," Emily instructed as she carefully set her embroidery on the table.

It seemed to take old Emmie forever to fetch a glass of water. He had time to return to his room, climb into bed, and make sure his little silver medal was safely tucked away in his pyjama shirt pocket. Finally Barney could see her shuffling along down the hallway.

"Here you go. Only a little now, I don't want you wetting the bed."

He accepted the shallow cup of water and took a sip.

"There we are. Now are you going to get to sleep like a good boy?"

He looked from the bonneted older woman to the closet door. It had been left open a crack again.

"Oh, for goodness sake, you'd think a quick boy your age would be past that now. There's nothing in there," she concluded her chastising with an irritated "tisk!" It was like watching a chicken, the flap of skin beneath her chin waggled and jiggled like she was an old hen.

He rolled over and pulled the covers over his shoulder.

"Oh for heaven's sake, I'll check this one last time but your parents will hear about this when they return from the country."

He watched through slitted lids as she shuffled to the closet. There was a scraping sound from within.

"What's this then?" Old Emmie asked herself. "Did you bring home a stray?"

The door burst open. He squeezed his eyes closed and covered his ears.

It was over in seconds, she didn't even have time to scream.

Barney waited a few moments longer and sighed as he got out of bed. He crossed his arms and walked to the closet door. "Still hungry?" he asked irritably.

The answer came in a whisper only he could hear.

"Okay, fine," he muttered as rolled his eyes and stomped out of the room. Before long he returned with Old Emmie's embroidery and needles. He tossed it into the closet and closed the door. "Maybe now I can get some sleep."

Randolph Lalonde is most well known for the Spinward Fringe Science Fiction series. He's also been caught dabbling in Fantasy and Horror from time to time, as evidenced by the piece presented above. He enjoys a quiet existence in Northern Ontario, where he lives with a tattoo artist and his lucky black cat. You can find out more about Randolph Lalonde's work by visiting www.randolphlalonde.com.

Angel of Death
Richard Gerard

The angel of death has come a-calling, and she is beautiful. To gaze upon her face would send a mortal soul to his grave, but I am already dying. She has come for me. To those like me, her presence brings a blessed tranquility; a happiness to be leaving this troubled world with the hope of something better.

I have seen her before, fleeting glimpses of her in my dreams. I have felt her around me for many years, her closeness calming my being. I do not know why she accompanied me throughout my life, but I was always happy to have her there. She has guided and protected me, her light a beacon in the night.

She has finally appeared before me, in all her glory. My time has come. In an instant, I know her story. I was but a child in this world when she passed away. I was her favorite. She chose to postpone her admission to heaven to look after me. She is not the angel of death, but my Guardian Angel, and she is beautiful. On her wings, we fly up to heaven.

Whether soft prose from a tender heart or a forlorn oration on humanity's depravity, Richard Gerard's poetry will make you feel. Look forward to his upcoming collection release and enjoy Angel of Death, before she calls on you.

The Frogs of Orange Tree

Christopher L. Hughes

It was a typical hot and steamy morning — then again, if you really thought about it, what would any critter think the weather was going to be like in August — it is Florida after all?

Shifty reached high into the air and stretched his front arms to knock out the kinks after a comfortable night's sleep, paying extra attention to knock the kinks out of his bulbous fingertips. It's the fingertips that are the most important, without the stick and the grip the ground comes into play very quickly! A frog's grip is essential for a frog's survival! He was pleased that it really was a good night's sleep, no attacks from birds, no stray cats sneaking around waking the family up, which meant waking him up as well. It was a nice night in August and Shifty was happy.

"Jumper, Lefty, time to get up!" Shifty's wife Greta called into the upper reaches of Orange Tree as the sun began to heat the leaves causing small wisps of steam to waft away in the still, humid air. Lefty stirred just for a moment and then abruptly flopped back down on his leaf pulling the makeshift leaf blanket over his head. Jumper didn't budge at all! It was the first day of school for the teenaged frogs and although they didn't show it, they were excited to go! It was their first day in Junior High, which meant they finally got to leave the humdrum lessons of elementary in Orange Tree and venture off to Live Oak at the corner of the yard! They were so excited last night that they had trouble falling asleep, which would explain the extremely lethargic state they were in right now!!

Shifty yelled! "Boys! Get up! Now!"

That's all it took! When dad yells, that means it's time to get moving! Jumper rolled over and nonchalantly hopped to the limb and started to the kitchen leaf while Lefty moved more cautiously. Lefty checked the upper reaches of the tree very carefully before making any sudden moves, as there were critters around who were not so friendly to tree frogs. A frog had to be specifically mindful of the black crows that harass all the residents of the community they call Orange Tree. Lefty knows all about the crows, after all, that is how he got his nick-name, "Lefty." He was fortunate that day two years ago that all he lost was his front right arm; it could have been a lot worse, he could have been somebody's lunch!

Mother frog Greta was setting out the bowls, impressive pieces made from hollow orange seeds and split in half, that contained various bugs and insects. As Lefty settled in above his bowl he found there was even a chunk of green worm in there! A special treat for their first day of school! Green worms are hard to get and are quite tasty!

Shifty quickly stabbed each and every morsel with his sticky tongue and gulped down his breakfast, oblivious to the fly's wing that was hanging awkwardly out the corner of his mouth. He was anxious to get off to work and since today was the day his boys were crossing the yard, he was a bit more nervous. Shifty is one of the crossing look-outs for the neighborhood. It is his job to monitor the north fence for danger as the frogs of Orange Tree moved from location to location in the Florida yard where they lived. It was a job he took quite seriously, he and his crew had not had any losses for over four years, and that frog wandered too far out of the safe zone and fell victim to the romping of the large white dog that lives here. Smashed into jelly!

"Now boys, listen up," Shifty firmly said as he leaned back on his hind legs and crossed his lanky arms over his chest. "The passage over to Live Oak can be very dangerous if you do not follow the rules. You can't wander, you can't lollygag and gawk at the surroundings, you need to get straight to Live Oak and into the boughs where your school is. I will be your monitor for the first part up until you pass the birdbath, after that Mr. Lumpy will see you safely to the trunk. Do you understand boys? It's exciting to leave Orange Tree, but it's also dangerous!"

The small frogs nodded in unison as the excitement built in their shiny green chests. The three said their goodbyes to a tearful Greta, her young frogs had never left Orange Tree before and she was both happy and fearful as they started their way down to the lower branches. When they reached the leaping platform at the base of the tree's trunk they gathered with other residents of Orange Tree who were waiting to make the passage.

"The cats are out!" an older-looking frog said as the three hopped over next to him. He turned his face, weathered and wrinkly, toward Shifty. "I've not seen the man-human yet, but all passage is suspended until they are back in the pool cage."

"That's smart thinking there Lumpy, the smaller one is quick! I've seen many a lizard packed off by that one! Where is the man-human anyway?"

"There!" Lumpy said with a nod of his head, "… on the patio with the newspaper, wait! Look over there! The bigger cat is about to jump the fence! The man-human will get him and hopefully take them both inside, that's what usually happens."

Sure enough, when the black cat hit the fence the man-human came out of the cage and herded both of the cats back in.

"Passage is open!" yelled Lumpy and he hopped off the perch and into the high grass, leaping to his watch post across the yard. He was soon followed by several other older frogs, each setting up as lookouts in their assigned positions. Shifty looked at his boys one more time, nodded and then winked, and then into the grass he went in one impressive hop.

The word was given to go! Jumper was the first of the young frogs to jump; Lefty was a bit more hesitant, giving one last look to the sky for any sign of crows. He knew that if the large birds could pluck a young frog out of a tree then they could surely snag one from the open ground of the yard. He was scared, he was nervous, but he needed to get over it! He jumped and started hopping to Live Oak with the others!

The passage went well, frogs were hopping, sentries were watching and it seemed that everyone was going to make it safely, another successful trip across the yard. Then suddenly a call through the air from the sentry closest to the birdbath!

"Blue Jay! Blue Jay on the fence!" was the cry.

The alarm now sounded, all the traveling frogs dropped in harmony and scrunched down into the grass remaining perfectly still. The yard was completely without movement as though no frogs or other creatures were anywhere to be found.

As fast as it came the bird flew away. The all clear was given and the trek resumed. All the frogs of Orange Tree made it safely to Live Oak; it was the start to an uneventful day!

Lefty and Jumper made it back to their branch in Orange Tree and Shifty came along soon after, his successful day as sentry complete! Their excitement of finally going to Junior High in Live Oak turned out to be as uneventful and boring as elementary school in Orange Tree! Where was all the fun they had heard about? Where were all the fancy new bugs and the cool surroundings? Live Oak turned out to be even more ugly than Orange Tree with its curled brown leaves and bothersome moss! It was not what they had expected and they were glad to be home. Both boys now dreamed of high school at Queen Palm, Queen Palm had to be better than Live Oak and Orange Tree put together, after all, that's where all the snobby tree frogs lived!

Their homework finished, the boys were perched neatly on their leaves alertly watching for any movement, waiting for an unsuspecting bug to happen by when suddenly Lefty hopped over to his dad and pointed to the big house!

"Dad, the curtains are open, hurry, we can see the picture thing for awhile!" Shifty quickly gathered the family and shuffled them to what they refer to as the 'picture watching' leaf, it was important for them to watch tonight, not because it was Thursday and their favorite show was playing on Animal Planet, no, it was important because there was a hurricane spinning in the Gulf of Mexico and Shifty wanted to know if it was heading their way!

As the frog family gathered on the leaf, Shifty handed out some gnats he had gathered earlier that day on his way home from work, a welcome and delicious snack for the frogs. Shifty wasn't as quick as he used to be in catching the little buggers so the snack was becoming more and more of a treat. As they munched on their gnats they stared across the pool through the sliding patio door just as the weatherman began pointing at the storm on the huge screen. Just then the man-human stood up! *NO!* Shifty thought! He had the changer thing in his hand; he was going to change the picture! "What about the hurricane?" Shifty hollered! "Greta, we really do need to find out how we can get one of those picture things in our tree, that man-human just wants to watch more man-humans playing with toys!"

Unexpectedly the man-human clicked off the picture thing and moved out of view of the frog family. Shifty was disappointed but couldn't dwell on it, it was the life of a tree frog and they were fortunate to allow their boys to experience anything human-related even if it was at the control of someone, or something, else. He reminded his boys again that some frogs, like those who live in Queen Palm or Live Oak don't even get the opportunity to see the picture thing, it is out of the view of their trees. So even a glimpse now and then was good for the boys, a new experience in this huge world!

The man-human reappeared from the big house off in the distance far beyond Live Oak and he was carrying some type of wooden panels. Shifty watched him intently, as all frog fathers do who live in Orange Tree, because he needed to be prepared to scramble the family if the man-human approached them. All frog families remember the tragedy six years ago when the man-human came with the machinery and cut down the entire Oleander neighborhood! Many tree frog families perished that day! It was horrible!

Shifty watched the man-human hammer the wood over the window, covering it completely. He watched as he did the same to another and then a third, he was covering the windows for some reason. Shifty was a smart tree frog and he could usually figure out what the man-human was doing, but this time he had no idea. As he watched the activity at the house he felt the slight change in the air, he felt the wind pick up; he noticed the absence of the sun, now obscured behind billowing gray clouds. He sure wished he knew what was happening with that hurricane!

Shifty continued to watch for the man-human, he could hear the hammering on the other side of the yard; apparently he was doing the same to all the windows of the entire big house. He taxed his tiny brain but just could not figure out what the man-human could be doing.

In the meantime Greta was tying things down that were now at the mercy of the increasing winds, they had already lost one of the leaf blankets, once it sailed away and fell to the ground it was considered lost.

Jumper was supposed to be helping his mother but suddenly his attention was drawn to the outer rim of branches. He saw another one, it was smaller than the first, same thorny spikes as the first but hopefully it would be easy to eat. He remembered his mom calling them spiny weavers or something like that, all Jumper knew is they had spikes, and they looked sharp! ... but a snack is a snack so he had to try and get it, that's what tree frogs do! He waited patiently, moving his tongue from side-to-side in his mouth, limbering up for the strike. He made his move! The spider turned away from him for just a moment and Jumper leaped to the next branch releasing his long elastic tongue as he flew through the air! He prepared his sticky fingers and hoped his aim was true. His slender fingers gripped the branch first, his hind legs landed and the worse possible thing that could have happened, happened! The branch broke! Jumper was falling! The branch was slamming into others, leaves were flying by and Jumper reached fruitlessly hoping to gain a grip and save himself from hitting the ground at full speed! His father's advice of always knocking the kinks out of your bulbous fingertips played over in his mind. *"It's the fingertips that are the most important,"* he always said! *"Without the stick and the grip the ground comes into play very quickly!"* Jumper was successful! The last branch before the ground was the one! He caught it with a gangly hand and held on! He was safe.

Greta and Shifty saw their boy fall and all they could do was hope for the best. All tree frogs were aware that once they hit the ground they were in danger, and the risk to other frogs coming to their aid was too high outside of the safe zone so it rarely happened, even if the fallen frog was family, that was just the way it was for tree frogs. They couldn't help him; all they could do was hope. They were relieved to see him snag the branch and was now hopping back to their home leaves in Orange Tree! They also noticed the wind was getting stronger and the sky was getting even darker!

There had never been a hurricane in this area that Shifty could recall and he wasn't really sure what he would do if this one hit them directly. He had convened with the other fathers of Orange Tree and even those that lived in Live Oak and no one had any clue of how intense a hurricane would be and where exactly they would go if one hit them. He did know that they were a powerful force and were not to be dismissed as simple storms, this he gathered while stealing glimpses of the weatherman on the picture thing. There was talk of the toads burrowing into the dirt to protect themselves, and Shifty considered that as an option, but that meant taking his family to the ground and facing the perils that existed there. He was quite sure that trying to stay in Orange Tree would be dangerous as some of the other families planned on doing. He didn't know much, but he knew that would be huge mistake!

The man-human was nowhere to be seen. The big house was now encased in wood and metal and Shifty did not know why. He had a funny feeling that it had to do with the hurricane but no one really knew and it wasn't until the heavy winds began to blow that Shifty figured it out. The man-human knew something that the tree frogs did not! The hurricane was coming! He was protecting his family inside the big house and when the wind blew a large piece of plastic that slammed into the covered window Shifty was convinced!

He carefully hopped to the branch where his family huddled, all three gripping and holding on tightly as Orange Tree swayed and tipped, all three closing their eyes to avoid the stinging rain. He gathered them together and told them they were making a run for it. They were going to seek shelter with the toads!

"Everyone! Listen to me!" he yelled to the other frogs of Orange Tree as they all huddled with their families, all gripping their branches! "This is a hurricane, we are in the middle of a hurricane! Orange Tree will not survive the force of the winds, we have all got to get out of the branches and burrow into the ground like the toads!"

"It's just a summer storm Shifty!" came the muffled call from another father through the whistling wind and the pounding rain! "It will blow over, they always do! We are staying put and riding it out!"

"No summer storm has ever moved Orange Tree like this, nor has the rain pelted us so fiercely Mr. Wartson, it is not a regular storm, you and your family are in great danger if you stay here! Please, all families of Orange Tree, come with us and burrow, it's the only chance we have to survive!"

The wind howled and the tree shook! Branches began to snap and limbs broke, shooting like mad hornets through the air! Shifty couldn't wait and try to talk sense into his fellow frogs! He carefully guided his family to the leaping platform, twice almost losing Lefty as the grip of his hind legs failed him, the lone hand and its sticky grip being the only thing that prevented him from being taken away in the wind. The second time being saved by the powerful grip of his father's bulbous fingers.

It was blowing too much now for the four of them to jump to the ground! They huddled on the platform, Greta and the boys waiting to see what Shifty wanted them to do. Suddenly a forceful gust caromed off the big house and lifted both Jumper and Lefty from their branch! Greta grabbed Jumper with both arms, her hind legs gripping the branch tightly, her holding on for her life with every available limb! At the same time Jumper grabbed Lefty by his dangling arm and the two boys were suspended in the forceful wind, their only lifeline the now failing grip of their mother. Shifty tightened his grip with his hind legs and when he felt he was as secure as he would ever be, he lunged out with his arms and grabbed both Lefty and Jumper! With all his might he pulled, he had to, this was his family, these were his boys! If he were to lose them now he would be devastated! He reached down into his soul with all he had and willed himself to find some hidden strength! He pulled harder fighting the massive force of wind, a wind like nothing he had ever experienced in his life! He gave one final yank! Lefty found a branch and grabbed it! Jumper also found a limb and wrapped his wet and bruised hands around it, allowing Greta to grab hold with all her limbs! They were all back on the platform!

"We have to get to the ground!" Shifty yelled, his words being taken away rapidly by the wind, him being unsure if he was even understood! "We will surely die if we stay in Orange Tree!"

He pointed to Greta's feet, "Hold on with your feet and grab the boys with your hands! Jumper, Lefty, all of us need to grab each other with our arms and then jump to the ground together!"

He and his family held each other tightly in a bundle as the grips with their feet began to fail each of them. "Jump!" Shifty yelled and released his grip! They all pushed off and sailed with the wind into the wooden fence behind what was left of Orange Tree! They hit hard and tumbled in a heap to the ground. Shifty heard his wife scream in pain and then saw the reason why! Her leg was broken! He made his way to her and pulled her to him. He wrapped his arms tightly and when he felt his boys nuzzle up next to them he had a small moment of happiness in this time of pain and disaster. They were all together! They were battered and beaten and he wasn't sure if they were even going to survive, but at least they were together!

His sight limited from the rain and the flying debris, Shifty pained to find an escape. The water was flowing past them rapidly and was beginning to rise, they wouldn't survive it, they would surely drown! Tree frogs did not swim, they did not know how!

Desperation was now taking its toll on the family of frogs from Orange Tree; they were not going to make it. It was during those last few moments that Shifty, through eyes now swollen with tears, took what he thought would be his final look at his family! He had failed to protect them! Now they were injured and beaten! He hated himself for not being prepared and tried to find a last bit of energy to move them, to try and save them, to try and get them away from this fence, out of this water and to safety! It was then that the croak caught his attention!

"Croak! Over here!" the voice called! "Croak! Tree Frogs, over here, quickly!"

Shifty lifted his head and through the pounding rain and stinging wind he saw the source of the call! A toad, waving them over to a cave at the side and bottom of the now shredded pool cage!

"Come Greta, we have to make it to the toads, can you bear the pain long enough to limp over there?"

Greta nodded but Shifty knew she was in no shape to limp anywhere. He held her in his arms and held on tightly; her injured leg dangling limply, he yelled to his boys to make their way to the toad's burrow. He put is head down, shielded his wife as best he could from the weather's onslaught, and trudged through the muck on two hind legs as he had seen the man-human do. He carried his wounded wife in his arms as Jumper and Lefty labored through the mud right behind. They made it to the burrow opening and as Greta was gently lifted from his arms and pulled inside by the massive toad, Shifty took one last look at the devastation! Orange Tree was completely stripped bare!

The toad poked his wart-covered head out of the hole and into the bright sunlight and the light breeze that accompanied it. The toads left the burrow and surveyed the damage to the yard they called home. Shifty and his boys also came out and all were heartbroken to find their home, the home to many tree frog families, completely stripped clean, nothing but a ragged, lichen-covered trunk in its place.

Greta joined them, her leg neatly set and stable by the skilled hands of the toads, and broke into heavy sobs and tears. All her friends were lost! Her home was gone! She gathered her family to her and looked at them as only a wife and mother could. She had an even fonder appreciation for the frog she took as a husband many years ago, he had saved them; he had saved his family from the disaster! They had nothing to return to but at least they had each other, that's more than could be said for the rest of the tree frogs.

As he and his family struggled back to the burrow and to the hospitality of the toads, Shifty felt a warming sensation build in his chest; he had made it, his family had made it! Looking at the devastation around him he found what mattered the most in their small part of the world, his family, and they made it through the hurricane!

Months had passed since Shifty, his wife Greta and their twin sons Jumper and Lefty endured the terrifying hurricane that almost cost them their lives. Greta was completely healed now and the tree frog family had said their goodbyes to the gracious family of toads that took them into their burrow when all on the surface was lost. The man-human had made many repairs, the screen around the pool, the damaged roof and the toppled fences were all fixed and back to normal. But what mattered the most to the frogs was their Orange Tree. It stood majestic before them; the healing well under way and fresh green leaves had populated the broken and shattered limbs. It was a bittersweet sight as there were no more frogs living in Orange Tree; they had all perished in the storm. Shifty and his family would be the first to repopulate, oh there will eventually be more, tree frogs from all over Florida will find their way here, but it will take time.

The family hopped to the base and stared up into the towering trunk, still covered with pale green lichens, as they prepared to jump to the platform to begin their renewed life. Suddenly the pool cage door swung open and the two black cats meandered out into the yard!

Shifty quickly ushered everyone up into the tree just as the smaller cat started to wiggle his behind and prepared to pounce! The family hopped and swung through the fresh boughs and branches and escaped yet another potential disaster. They were home! They were the frogs of Orange Tree once again.

The End

Christopher L. Hughes is the author of the fantasy Trilogy – Grinzleville - and the new historical adventure – That's Ancient History. He writes in the middle-grade fantasy and adventure genre in which this short story – The Frogs of Orange Tree – can be included. All Christopher's works can be found at http://www.openingdaymedia.net

The Land of Fear
William Woodall

Wisdom is better than weapons of war.
                                    - Ecclesiastes 9:18

Once there was a girl named Elisabeth, who had a most amazing adventure.

She lived in a cottage with her father and two sisters (their names were Aline and Celeste), in the village of Brumbling, not far from the River of Fear. Now this was a terrible place where only the bravest or the most foolish people ever dared to go, for no one had ever returned.

All sorts of things were whispered about it by the people of Brumbling. Some believed that there must be a dragon, and others spoke of a terrible sorcerer in a tall black tower. A few told stories of things even more frightening. But everyone also agreed that there was a treasure so wonderful and amazing that it could not even be described.

Elisabeth had heard these things all her life long, and she burned with desire to know the real truth of the matter.

In those days a great war had come to Brumbling, and the village stood almost empty. Elisabeth was not old enough to help, and she had been left in the village with her older sisters to tend the fields and the house. Their father was an excellent bowman, and had gone away with the army for a little while. Elisabeth knew that it was necessary, but she still felt lonely without Father.

For one thing, Aline and Celeste were not very kind to her. They seemed to think that Elisabeth should do all the nasty, tedious chores that they didn't want to do, and Aline especially would pinch her unmercifully. Elisabeth endured all this until the day the town crier ran through the village, shrieking that the barbarians had defeated the army of Brumbling, and that they now demanded a mountain of gold from the people by the end of the day, or they would utterly destroy the village at sunrise tomorrow morning.

Aline and Celeste wept and screamed when they heard this news, and immediately began packing bags to run as far away as possible. Elisabeth was angry with them for being so cowardly, and told them so. But

Celeste only threw a bag at her and told her not to be a fool, and Aline pinched her arm hard enough to leave bruises.

Elisabeth made up her mind that she would not run away from the barbarians with her sisters. She decided that she would herself get the mountain of gold that they demanded, by going into the forbidden lands near the River to find the treasure.

Therefore she packed the bag Celeste had given her, but instead of waiting for her sisters, she slipped quietly out the back door and ran to the barn. The hay loft was nearly full with fresh straw, and Elisabeth hid herself quite carefully in the darkest corner she could find. Aline and Celeste never visited the barn if they could help it, for they hated to get dirty, and Celeste especially was afraid of the cows. Elisabeth herself rather liked the animals. She had spent many mornings feeding them and collecting the milk.

It wasn't long before she heard Aline calling her name, and shortly after that she heard her sister's footsteps running into the byre.

"Beth!" she called, so loud that Elisabeth could imagine her standing right under the hay loft. She kept very quiet until she heard Aline go away. That didn't take long, for she knew Aline wouldn't spend any more time looking for her than she had to.

As soon as she was sure Aline was gone,

Elisabeth left the barn and walked briskly to the little creek that flowed behind her house. It was not much more than ten feet across, and she immediately began to follow it downstream, for she knew it would lead her to the river before too long. That was a good thing, for she had no wish to become lost in the woods on her way there.

Indeed it wasn't very long at all before the creek entered the edge of the forest and lost itself among the tall dark trees. Elisabeth had never been inside the forest before, for it was far too near the river for anyone's comfort, and there were the most horrifying stories told about what went on there.

One of these stories in particular was on Elisabeth's mind as she looked at the opening. Her Tante Cheri had told her, long ago, that there were ghouls that haunted the woods, hideous beasts wrapped in rotting grave clothes who waited with dripping mouths to kill and eat anyone who ventured into the darkness under the trees. Elisabeth had pretended not to be scared at the time, but now she couldn't help wondering if there might not really be something in there after all. The woods looked very dark and scary.

However, while she hesitated at the edge, she suddenly heard the very last thing she wanted to hear.

"Beth!" came Celeste's voice, somewhere not too far behind her. Elisabeth made up her mind quickly. Without even looking back to see how close Celeste might be, she took off running toward the woods as fast as she could go. She could move very quickly when she wanted to, and it was no more than a few seconds before she felt the trees close in around her. She didn't stop even then, but continued running along the creek bank until the edge of the woods was far behind her. Celeste would never follow her among the trees, of that she was certain. She hadn't forgotten about the ghouls, but she was determined to go ahead anyway.

The creek gurgled and bubbled placidly along beside her while she walked, and after a few hours (during which she saw no ghouls at all), Elisabeth came abruptly to the bank of the river. The creek flowed out past a little cottonwood tree and lost itself in the main current, so that she now had no path to follow.

There was a sort of beach at the place where she stood, of rocks and sand. The river was nothing special, as far as Elisabeth could tell. There was certainly nothing scary or unusual about it. Since she had come back out into the daylight, the whole idea of ghouls and magic had begun to seem rather silly again. She looked up and down the bank without seeing anything to give her a goal to move toward, so she sat down on the warm sand to think about it a while.

Elisabeth had often gone down to the creek to play in the sand or skip rocks on the water if she could find any good ones, and she began absentmindedly tossing pebbles into the river while she thought about what to do. The current must have been swift, for it snatched away the ripples almost as soon as they formed. She hadn't been doing this for very long when a huge silver fish came to the top of the water and looked at her.

"I do wish you would quit dropping rocks into my bedroom," the fish growled, in a bubbly, fishy sort of voice.

"I'm sorry. . . I didn't know you were there," Elisabeth said, too startled to think of anything else to say.

"What?! You didn't know that fishes live in the river?" the fish demanded, insulted.

"No. . . I mean yes, I did know that; I just never thought about it before," Elisabeth admitted.

"Humph," the fish grumbled, "Well, I forgive you just this once, since you're only a girl and couldn't possibly be expected to know any better, but it had best not happen ever again."

Now Elisabeth thought the fish was being very rude, and she stood up to tell him so, but just as she reached the edge of the water she twisted her ankle on a loose stone and fell down. It hurt fairly badly, and she began to rub it.

"Tsk, tsk. . . clumsy as well as stupid," the fish commented, watching her. Elisabeth lost her patience, for she disliked rude and insensitive people.

"You could at least ask if I was alright. I might have broken my ankle, you know," she told him disapprovingly.

"But you didn't, now did you?" he asked her cheerfully, as if that solved the whole matter. She was still trying to think how to reply to such a question when the fish went on without waiting for her answer.

"Still, you might have an idea. That could be a nasty bruise later on. I'd better get you something for it," he said, almost to himself. Before she could reply, he disappeared under the water again.

The fish wasn't actually gone very long, but Elisabeth did have time to stand up and put some weight on her ankle. The pain was too much to bear, and it forced her to sit down again. Before long the fish reappeared, holding a thin sliver of what looked like beaver wood in its mouth. He spit it out on the beach, then coughed up a bit of mucus and blew it into the water. Elisabeth looked at him with disgust.

"Well, are you going to pick up the stick, or what?" the fish asked her impatiently. Truthfully, Elisabeth would rather have had nothing else to do with the fish, but she decided that if he meant to help her she ought to be polite. She reached out and picked up the beaver stick. It was still slimy from the fish's mouth and from whatever nasty place it had been taken from. She held it with distaste.

"Well, aren't you going to use it?" the fish demanded.

"What's it for, and how am I supposed to use it?" she asked, getting annoyed herself now.

"I would have thought even a little girl would know what to do with *that*," the fish told her. She could almost imagine him rolling his eyes at her. . . if he had had any eyelids.

"But never mind. Touch the stick to your ankle," he told her. Elisabeth did so, and instantly the pain disappeared. She stood up carefully to test it out, and to her surprise she found that her ankle was completely well again. She looked up at the fish.

"Thank you," she told him, and meant it.

"Well. . . I couldn't have a litterbug lolling around on my doorstep all day," the fish muttered. Elisabeth was willing to tolerate his gruffness now, so she let it pass. She started to hand him back the stick.

"No, no. . . you keep it, missie. I don't need it anymore," he grumbled. Elisabeth slipped the stick into her pocket and fastened the button, and while she was thinking about what else to say to the fish, he suddenly disappeared back into the river, without so much as a flick of his tail to say goodbye.

"Well, Mr. Fish, I'll certainly remember not to throw any more rocks into your bedroom," she said to herself, looking at the spot where the fish had disappeared. A few bubbles were coming up from somewhere below, but she couldn't tell if he heard her or not.

After a while, Elisabeth realized she couldn't stand on the bank all day. She had to find some way to keep going. Upstream was a thicket of bamboo, which looked so tangled and heavy that she doubted she could ever get through it. Behind her was the ghoul-haunted forest, and she was still uneasy about going back in there. Ahead of her was the river, much too wide and strong to think of swimming.

"And so," she said to herself, "that really leaves only one way left. Downstream it is." In that direction the rocky beach went on for quite some time, and Elisabeth followed it. Now and then she had to stop and dump sand and pebbles out of her shoes, but otherwise the going was not too difficult.

Eventually, though, she came to a knot of wild thorn trees that completely blocked the way. Elisabeth was not anxious to go in among the thorn trees, because they were wickedly sharp. The river looked a bit shallower near the edge, and she decided after much thought to try wading in the shallows until she got past the thorn thicket. Then maybe she could continue on her way.

She took off her shoes and held them so they wouldn't get wet, and then gingerly stepped into the water. It was warm as summer, not freezing cold as she had half expected it would be. The bottom seemed to be mostly gravel in that place, which made it easy to keep her footing.

Not quite easy enough, though. She had made it most of the way around the thorn thicket when she lost her balance and fell into the deep water with a huge splash. The current snatched her at once, and almost before she knew what was happening it had carried her far from the shore. She lost her shoes and tried her best to swim toward the bank, but the swirling river was too strong, and she was getting farther away from land every second.

Elisabeth began to get frightened, and that is always a very bad thing to do when one is swimming. But before she could get really terrified, she felt her feet drag the bottom for just a second, and she turned her head to see an island right behind her.

Elisabeth wasted no time forgetting about the distant shore. She could reach the island, and that was all she cared about.

She grabbed a muddy root that hung out into the water and hung on for dear life. The current tried to tear her away, but gradually she was able to pull herself along the root until she reached the shore. She climbed up out of the water, soaking wet and shivering in the light breeze.

The island wasn't very big. In fact, it was barely more than a sand bar with a few tough bushes growing on it. Elisabeth looked out across the river and immediately gave up all hope of swimming back to the bank she'd just come from. It was much too far, and the river was too swift.

She crossed the island and found that it wasn't nearly so far to the bank on that side. Only about a hundred feet of sluggish backwater separated the island from solid ground. But that way was choked with fallen logs and brush that didn't look appealing at all. Elisabeth knew she couldn't stay on the island forever, but how was she to get off?

She was staring at the log jam, wondering if she might possibly risk walking across it, when she got a nasty surprise.

"Hello, miss. Can I help you?" a cheerful voice asked her. Elisabeth was startled, and looked down at her feet to see an alligator floating in the water. He was much too close to her feet for comfort, and Elisabeth stepped back hastily. The alligator giggled. Not a deep laugh like you might have expected, but a high-pitched giggle that reminded Elisabeth of her sisters in one of their silliest moods.

"Surely you're not afraid, are you?" it asked her, and giggled again.

"Um. . . just a little bit," Elisabeth admitted, for she was a very truthful girl. The alligator stopped giggling to itself and looked at her for a long time.

"Hmm. . . . no, I don't think you'd make more than a mouthful, so you need not be afraid," it told her. Elisabeth didn't like that answer much, but she thought it was best not to argue. The alligator might change its mind.

"I need to get across the river," she told him, changing the subject.

"I'd be glad to give you a lift over the water," the alligator said brightly, with a toothy smile that didn't do anything at all to make Elisabeth feel better. While she hesitated, the alligator went on without waiting for an answer.

"What are you doing here by the river, anyway? We don't often get human beings down this way," he said.

"An army of barbarians has invaded my village, and they want a mountain of gold or they'll destroy everything. So I came here to find it," she told him.

"Hmm. . . well now that's not very nice of them, is it? No, not nice at all," the gator giggled.

"It's not really very funny," Elisabeth scolded him.

"Ah, no, no, I suppose it isn't," the gator agreed, still smirking. Elisabeth was about to decide the alligator was just as annoying as the fish had been, if that was possible. But the fish had helped her, and maybe the alligator could help her too.

"Do you know where I could find any gold?" she asked him hopefully.

"Ah, gold! No, there's no gold anywhere near the river. We have no use for that sort of thing," he declared. Elisabeth was crushed, for it seemed that her trip to the river was a huge waste of time after all, and tears began to fall from her eyes into the water.

"Ah, missie, you mustn't cry now," the alligator told her hastily. Elisabeth lost her patience.

"The barbarians will destroy my village if they don't get that gold. Why shouldn't I cry about that?" she demanded hotly. The gator seemed taken aback for a moment, but he soon regained his composure. He giggled again, which irritated Elisabeth to no end.

"Well now, I might be able to tell you something useful about that, I might. I just might," he said, smiling mysteriously. He was obviously enjoying himself very much. Elisabeth stopped crying and waited for him to tell her what it was, but he didn't say a word.

"What was it you could tell me?" she finally asked, when the silence had stretched out for a minute or more.

"I thought you'd never ask!" the gator exclaimed, with another attack of giggles.

"It's true there's no gold in this place, but there's something much better," he whispered. Elisabeth was interested now and leaned close to hear better.

"What is it?" she asked.

"On the far bank of the river, a little downstream, there's a ruined stone tower. And in a room at the top of that tower there lives a huge snowy owl. And if you bring him something he likes well enough, he can grant you a wish. Anything you want. Even a mountain of gold," the gator informed her. Elisabeth was overjoyed at that news, and her face lit up. The gator saw it.

"Ah, not so fast, missie! If you go to the owl emptyhanded, or if you bring him something he doesn't like, then he'll eat you for supper instead of giving you a wish," the alligator warned her. That did put a crimp in things, Elisabeth had to admit. She wasn't ready to give up yet, though.

"What does the owl like?" she asked.

"No one has ever figured that out. Only one man ever came back out of the tower alive, and he isn't talking," the gator told her, nodding mysteriously again.

"Where can I find that man? Why won't he talk to anybody?" she demanded.

"Because, when he came out from visiting the owl he tried to cross the river, and I ate him up," the gator told her with another one of those toothy smiles. Elisabeth stepped back from the shore in sudden alarm. The gator slipped into another attack of giggles, so much so that he choked on a mouthful of water and had to cough.

"Just pulling your leg, missie," he told her, when he was able to contain himself.

"That wasn't funny," she scowled.

"Ah, but it was! But truly, I'll be glad to give you a ride across the water on my back, if you like," he offered again.

Elisabeth honestly didn't like that idea at all, but she couldn't think of any other way to get off the island. She had to get to the owl. As soon as she figured out what would keep him from eating her for supper, that was. So she gathered her courage and climbed on the alligator's back. He faithfully carried her across the river as he said he would, and deposited her on the shore. She was glad to be on solid ground again.

"Just follow the river downstream, and you'll come to the tower before long!" he called out as he swam away, and giggled again. Elisabeth watched him until he disappeared, and then set off down the bank. Walking barefoot slowed her down considerably, and she wished she hadn't lost her shoes.

Even so, it wasn't very long before she saw a black stone tower rising above the trees near the bank, just as the alligator had said she would. There she stopped, because she had no idea what the owl might like. What could she give him that he didn't already have?

It was also still daylight, and she remembered that owls liked to sleep during the day. She certainly didn't want to annoy him by waking him up early. So in the meantime she sat down on a dead log to wait.

By the time it started to get dark she still hadn't thought of any good answer to the question of what to give the owl, and she was afraid he would soon leave the tower to go hunting for the night. Elisabeth knew there wasn't time to wait and think about it any longer. The barbarians would destroy Brumbling at sunrise if they didn't have the gold by then.

She therefore decided to go in and speak to the owl boldly, and try to make a deal with him. She hadn't forgotten what the alligator said about being eaten for supper, but that was a risk she decided she'd just have to take.

She approached the tower slowly, not eager at all to face the owl any sooner than she had to. There was a door in the base of the tower which seemed to be the only way in, and at first she was afraid it would be locked. But when she touched it, she soon discovered that it was made of wood so rotten that she could pull it apart with her bare hands. She tore down enough of the door to squeeze through, and found herself in an open room that took up the entire bottom floor of the tower. There was a stone staircase that circled the outer wall and led up through the ceiling, and she knew that had to be where the owl lived. She took a deep breath to calm her fear and then very resolutely climbed up to meet him.

There were three floors to the tower, and when she reached the top one, Elisabeth found the owl. He was sitting on a nest made of branches and straw, looking out into the gathering dusk through a big ragged hole in the stone wall. He was white as snow, and he had to have been at least the size of a horse. His eyes were big as dinner plates, and his beak looked sharper than a knife, with a cruel hook on the end. He must have heard her coming up the stairs, for he turned to look at her when she came in.

"Why have you come here?" he asked, getting right to the point. For a moment Elisabeth was too terrified to speak, but at last she found her voice.

"Sir Owl, I'm sorry to disturb you. But an army has attacked my village, and they will destroy it this very sunrise unless we give them a mountain of gold. I came here because I was told that you could do this, if I wished it," she said, in a voice that she hoped sounded braver than she felt. The owl studied her with its dinner-plate eyes for a while.

"Not many are brave enough to come here and ask, but yes, I could do that. But surely you know the price. What have you brought me?" he said at last. This was the moment Elisabeth had been dreading.

"Sir Owl, I had no idea what you might wish for, but if there's anything I have or can get for you, I will do it," she told him. The owl looked impatient.

"Now don't tell me you're one of *those* kind," he said in disgust. Then he seemed to think better of it.

"As a matter of fact there *is* something I want, but you could never get it for me. It lies at the bottom of the river, and the current is very deep and strong. Since you came here for someone else's sake and not for greed, I'll let you go without eating you tonight, but don't bother me again," the owl told her, and then turned as if to go. Elisabeth couldn't let her only chance slip away.

"Sir Owl, what is this thing you want? I promise I'll find a way to get it for you!" she cried. The owl looked back at her in annoyance.

"Still here? I thought I told you to go away before I eat you," he growled.

"I have to know what will save my village," she told him, not backing down.

"You're a plucky one," he commented, half to himself. "Alright then, girl. If you're so sure of yourself then I'll tell you what I want, and if you can bring it here before the night is over then I'll grant your wish. But if not, then I'll find you and eat you for breakfast, no matter where you may try to hide. Will you make that deal?" he demanded.

"Yes sir," she told him without hesitation. He looked amazed, but he didn't try to talk her out of it anymore. He simply began to tell her what she needed to know.

"Long ago, I had a magical piece of wood that kept me young and strong at all times, and it could heal any sickness or injury there was. But as I flew across the river one night, another owl attacked me by surprise. He thought he could kill me and take my tower and my magic. How the feathers flew in the moonlight! I ate him for supper that night. But during the fight I dropped my stick in the river, and without it I'll soon grow old and weak, and then another owl will take my place after all. But no one can dredge it up from the bottom of the river, even if it hasn't been washed down to the sea. You won't be able to do it either, but maybe you'll taste better than a deer or a goat in the morning," the owl said.

Elisabeth shivered, but she reached in

the pocket of her dress, thankful indeed for the button that held it shut.

"Is this what you want, Sir Owl?" she asked, pulling out the stick she'd gotten from the fish. The owl gasped when he saw it, which sounded very strange.

"Where did you find that? Give it to me at once!" he cried. Elisabeth held out the stick so the owl could grasp it in one of his razor-sharp talons. He snatched it from her as fast as he could get close enough, as if afraid she might change her mind. When he managed to contain his pleasure, he looked at her again.

"Well! You lived up to your end of the bargain, so now I must live up to mine. You get just one wish, missie, so take care! Use it wisely," he told her.

"Then I wish for a mountain of-" she began, but the owl interrupted her.

"I'll offer you a bit of advice, missie, and if you're wise then you'll take it. Don't ask for that mountain of gold, because if you do then who's to say the barbarians will keep their word? They may take the gold and destroy the village anyway. And even if they don't, then another enemy may appear someday, or another disaster may come. Think of more than just today," he urged her. Elisabeth saw that this was good advice, but it left her wondering what she should ask for.

"What should I wish for then?" she finally asked the owl.

"Hoo. . . no one has ever asked me that before," he told her, seeming surprised.

"But I need to know," she insisted.

"Then ask for wisdom, missie. Because wisdom is the chief thing, and if you have that, then everything else will fall into place," he told her. It seemed just like the sort of thing an owl would say.

"Then I wish to be the wisest person in the world," she said. The owl couldn't smile with his beak, but Elisabeth was certain she could hear it in his voice when he spoke.

"Your wish is granted. And because you trusted me and asked for the best thing of all, I will destroy your enemies myself," he told her.

And it was so. Elisabeth made her way back to Brumbling with no further adventures the next day, and she found that all the barbarians had been destroyed or driven away during the night, just as the owl had promised her.

No one thought to ask where Elisabeth had been. No one except Celeste, that is, who had seen her go into the forest. But when Celeste pressed her to know what she had seen and done, Elisabeth would only smile and say nothing.

Thus it was that no one in Brumbling

ever knew that Elisabeth had saved them from the barbarians at the risk of her life, and she was content to have it so. But in later years, her wisdom was such that the people often came to her for help with their most difficult problems, and they were often amazed at the words that came from her mouth.

In time, her fame spread even to other villages, so that there were always visitors at the little cottage who wished to speak with her. Many of the visitors were wealthy and important people, and left rich gifts at her feet. And at last she was held in such awe by the people of many lands that no one would have dreamed of attacking Brumbling ever again. Thus it happened even as the owl had told her it would; by asking for wisdom, she had received wealth and honor and power as well, without even needing to ask.

And Elisabeth lived a long and happy life in blessedness.

William Woodall is the author of two fantasy novels for young adults, including *The Prophet of Rain,* and more recently *Cry for the Moon.* He is a teacher, counselor, and father of three. His work is often inspirational in nature, as he likes happy endings. This story was written for his daughter, and here he explores the relationship between love and courage. This story also appears in the collection *Beneath a Star-Blue Sky.*

You can find William online at http://www.williamwoodall.org

Sam

K.A. Thompson

Whenever I think of Sam I picture him standing in front of the big bay window, staring out at the snow, watching as it piled in huge clumps on his front lawn, the tree limbs heavy and white. He bitched and moaned about the cold and the sidewalks to be shoveled, yet when the first hints of winter brushed by he always waited eagerly for that first flake to strike the ground, for the air to fill with sights and smells of winter. He reveled in the watercolor gray of the skies, little boys wading through knee deep snow with their dogs and sleds in tow, snowmen dotting the streets and soft angels drawn impulsively just outside his front door.

There were the other things in life that Sam hated as intently as snowflakes dancing through the skies onto his sidewalks; the sounds of his daughter's awkward fingers tinkering over the piano keys, relentlessly, pursuing the perfection of *Twinkle Twinkle Little Star*, banana breath and sticky fingers reaching over the edge of the mattress to greet him just minutes before the alarm was set to go off; his two-year-old son gleefully peeing up the wall behind the toilet, squealing with delight at the discovery of this simple ability. There were all the odd, quirky things that irritated and aggravated him that he kept tucked away in some private place deep inside.

Sam also hated his job, contending with all those sparks of curiosity flying from the eyes and minds of ultra absorbent five-year-old boys and girls, living through story hour and the wonders of science and, most important, Show and Tell. In ten years of silently suffering the kindergarten moppets, Sam had been Shown and Told it all. He hated all the laughter, recess patrol, listening as some mirthful prodigy reeled off his first ever joke.

"Mr. Moore, why does a lion eat raw meat? He can't cook!"

"Mr. Moore, why did the scientist turn off his doorbell? He wanted to win the No-bell prize!"

"Mr. Moore, what'dya get when you pour boiling water down a rabbit hole? Hot cross bunnies!"

Oh, Sam hated it all.

The children, the laughter, all the little firsts. They were too much like snowflakes. There once in a brilliant flash of beauty, and then gone.

"I know *Green Eggs and Ham* backwards and forwards," Sam sighed, a twist of tired laughter tinging his voice. "It's the first thing I read them during the year, and for the next week I'm Sam-I-Am."

"You tell them your first name?"

Sam popped open a Diet Coke, leaning back in one of the cheap metal chairs provided in the teachers' lounge. He nodded as he took a sip, looking at his new student teacher; this was the first time Sam could remember being assigned a male student. "No reason not to. It makes me human. They call me Mr. Moore, but they know that deep down I'm just plain Sam."

"So I should introduce myself as Tim?"

"Up to you. I usually introduce myself as Mr. Moore, and then tell them my first name is Sam."

"And then you pull out *Green Eggs and Ham*?"

"Exactly."

"'I do not like them Sam-I-Am.'"

"Be honest. Have you ever had green eggs and ham?"

"Not in this lifetime."

"Don't knock it till you've tried it.

Theodore Geisel never wrote crap, you know."

Tim Anderson frowned. "Who?"

"Dr. Seuss." Sam took another swallow of the Coke. What human didn't know about Dr. Seuss? "This is kindergarten, Timothy. Seuss is the icon of great literature here. These kids know every book, every line, word for word. If you want to survive, so will you." He reached into his brief-case and pulled out a well-worn copy of *Horton Hears a Who*.

"Memorize this by tomorrow, Mr. Anderson. And then read it like you mean it."

The simple fact that he could reel off, line by line, with great dramatic inflection, nearly every single word of every single book written by Dr. Seuss, bothered Sam. His intention had been to fill their little minds with great facts of literature and mathematics and science. His reality was that *The Cat In The Hat* was high literature in the rugrat set, math was limited to memorization of numbers through ten, their phone numbers and addresses, and science was the wonder of how to make everlasting soap bubbles and volcanoes out of baking soda, vinegar, and old newspapers.

He could explode the entrails out of any paper-mache volcano better than any other teacher in school.

His soap bubbles expanded and floated

endlessly, disappearing out of sight before they popped.

He taught his students their colors and their numbers through song, he taught them how to write their first and last names, he taught them simple addition by using pennies they could keep when they solved the problem correctly.

The kids got rich.

Sam got tired. Very tired.

Sam, after ten years of cajoling young minds to open up, ten years of nursing hurt feelings and playing at recess and singing goofy songs at the top of his lungs, was ready to quit.

He hated it.

Really.

"Parent-teacher conferences," he told Tim, "are one of the necessary evils. Most of the mothers and fathers are alright—" he shrugged and sighed, "—there are the few demon seeds.

"'What?'" he went on, voice pitched high. "'Not little Johnny. Little Johnny is a genius, a perfect angel.'"

He crumpled his Coke can with one hand and sent it sailing across the room, landing neatly into the metal wastebasket. "I hate to tell you, lady," he said, mostly to himself, "but your little Johnny is saddled with so much of your cast-off emotional baggage that he's turning into a five-year-old walking S.O.B. headed straight for juvenile hall, if he's lucky."

Tim sat quietly, not sure what to say.

Sam looked up at him, smiling sadly. "You know what really bites? Deep down Little Johnny is probably a good kid. A redeemable kid. But Mom the alcoholic and Dad the workaholic don't even recognize the pot of gold living under their inebriated noses..."

Sam didn't always hate things. Sam at twenty-two was an idealist, full of life and ideas and was sure he could turn the world upside down.

Sam at thirty-two realized the world had already been turned upside down, and he didn't like the way things scattered.

"When I first started this," he confided to his wife, late at night in the comfort of a completely dark room, "I wanted to give them the universe. Every little bit of wonder and every piece of magic."

"You still can."

Sam stood by the bedroom window, staring out at the night sky and the stars that winked back at him. "No," he sighed, "not really. Most of them don't want to know and those who do ... they're too young to understand."

"Those little minds understand more than you realize."

Sam nodded. "Brains like little sponges," he agreed. "But that's not it, not really. They need something else. Something I'm not sure is in me anymore."

Sam had known his fair share of gifted five-year-olds. Kids who grasped the concept of addition beyond the simple chanting of "One plus one equals two. Two plus two equals four." The pleasant surprises that came to him wrapped in brand new sneakers and jeans a size too big rarely stayed throughout the school year. They showed up in his classroom, their little heads already filled with the standard kindergarten education, and after a few weeks of trying to reach through their clouds of boredom, Sam reluctantly sent them on their way to first grade.

Deep down he knew it was for the best; the children weren't there to appease his ego as an educator. He understood that they were there to learn, and that he had a responsibility to teach the curriculum for the rest of his students.

But those rare prodigies, those were the students who most fascinated Sam. They gave him a glimpse into the futures of the rest of his kids. He had the chance to see how a young mind could progress and thrive.

Sam rarely saw his former students, other than passing them in the hallways or the cafeteria. He never knew if he'd given them the foundation he wanted and they needed, not unless one of their later teachers came asking questions. Consulting Sam was rare.

Sam often stood on the playground during recess to watch the kids play. There were, he told Tim, other adults hired to do that, and he could spend his time better by preparing for the afternoon class, or the next day, but he thought he might know them better as individuals by the way they played.

And sometimes, when the weather was good and the attendants brought out the big red rubber balls, Sam played a low key game of dodge ball with them.

"It doesn't have to last long. Just be their target for ten minutes, and they'll be happy the rest of the day."

But Sam hated the squeals of laughter. Seriously.

Almost six months before Sam began to hate it all, on a bright winter day, just long enough after the holidays that the kids had begun to settle down, Sam welcomed a new student into his already overcrowded classroom.

Shane Hamilton eased into this new environment as if he had been there all along. He was friendly and instantly well-liked – a gregarious six year old, Sam mused – and brighter than any child Sam had seen in years.

He waffled over what to do with Shane; it was too late in the year to shove him out the door on his way to first grade. There was nothing he was teaching that Shane didn't already know, yet the boy never stared at him with glazed over, disinterested eyes. Shane didn't fidget with boredom or talk out of turn; he completed worksheets without complaint, quietly read books while others were still working, and never whined about how little there really was for him to do.

"He could be learning much more with a private tutor," Sam explained to Shane's mother. "Keeping him here is holding him back."

Sam Moore's kindergarten class, Mrs. Hamilton insisted, was exactly where Shane wanted to be.

Sam left it alone. If Shane's mother wanted him to flounder in kindergarten, far be it for him to interfere. He welcomed Shane's presence in his world from 12:30 to 3:30 every day. He simply didn't want to let the boy down.

At the end of Shane's first month in his class, Sam discovered that he was as musically gifted as he was academically. He'd sat quietly through countless other days of Show and Tell, but on a day when a hint of spring warmth was seeping through the last days of winter cold, Shane brought his guitar to school. He was the last to stand up in front of the class, and when he did he explained, in simple terms, all the parts of the guitar his father had given him when he was four years old.

On request, Shane began to play. He plucked out smooth versions of kid-friendly songs his classmates knew, and for the next half-hour the room full of five- and six-year-old kids happily sang along.

"Mr. Moore," someone asked, "can you play?"

Sam shook his head. "I never learned to play anything. I always wanted to, though."

Shane held his guitar out to his teacher, and offered to teach him two or three chords. Egged on by the pint-sized crowd, Sam couldn't refuse. He learned three basic chords and clumsily plucked them out while the kids sang *Row, Row, Row Your Boat*.

"When you grow up," he told Shane, "you should be a teacher. You're pretty good at it."

It was the first time Sam saw a smile slide from Shane's face.

Worried that simple subtraction would bore Shane out of his mind, Sam borrowed workbooks from first and second grade teachers, and quietly set about teaching Shane math more complicated than his classmates were being introduced to. While they filled out their worksheets – not as quietly as Sam would have liked – Shane sat in a small chair beside Sam's desk, easily grasping the addition and subtraction of double digits, and he took to basic multiplication with ease.

"If we time it right," Sam said to Mrs. Hamilton after class, "he'll be prepared to go directly into second grade next year."

"We'll see," was her non-committed reply. "Shane may wish to stay with his friends."

Sam wanted to argue – if Shane was ever going to skip a grade, now was the time to do it – but she smiled brightly, took her son by the hand, and walked away.

Some evenings, Sam watched his baby son squirming in the play pen, and wondered what Shane's parents had done to foster their son's intelligence. He listened to his three-year-old daughter giggle as she played with her dolls, and wondered if, whatever it was, it was too late to begin with her.

"Maybe," his wife said, "they did nothing special, and Shane is just an exceptionally bright kid."

Sam allowed for that possibility, and wondered if he'd had students in the past who blossomed as well once they moved beyond the confines of kindergarten.

It wasn't ego, he told himself, but he deeply, truly, hoped there were many.

Shane missed his first day of school in early spring, when dripping noses and hacking coughs were so much a part of the background static of his classroom that Sam only noticed if one of the kids sounded as if they might cough up a significant body part. He dismissed his prize pupil's absence as another spring cold, and went about teaching the rugrat form of botany.

"Today," he informed the class, "we're going to plant sunflower seeds, and after they start to grow you can take them home and plant them in your yard."

The excitement that vibrated off his students grew when he told them, in a voice near a whisper, "They can grow over six feet tall!"

The parents would be less than thrilled.

They would get over it.

When Shane missed an entire week of school, Sam worried and asked the receptionist in the front office to call his home and see how he was doing.

She reported to him later in the day that Shane was better, and would be back in class in a day or two. Sam thought it was a long time to keep a kid home for a cold, but he respected his parents for not exposing the rest of the class to it; he wished more parents were as considerate.

Shane, pale and with dark circles under his eyes, was back in school two days later; he brought his guitar again for Show and Tell, mostly because he had learned two new chords and wanted to teach them to Sam.

"Someday," he said to Shane, "I'm going to get a guitar of my own and practice, so that I can show *you* a new chord."

Shane grinned and then snorted, "You'll never be that good."

Two weeks later Shane was again absent from class. Instead of asking the receptionist to call about him, Sam picked up the phone himself, waited through an abysmally long answering machine message, and left a quick one of his own.

Worried about Shane. Let me know if he needs anything. Call me at home, 555-4813.

He didn't expect anyone to call.

Perhaps Shane was just a sickly kind of kid.

Twenty minutes after Shane's father called, Sam was standing in the corridor outside a hospital room, listening as Shane's father spoke in hushed tones. He glanced frequently into the room where Shane was curled up on his side, eyes closed, tubes attached to his arms with wide stretches of white tape.

"He wanted to go to school," Mr. Hamilton explained. "After we got his prognosis we thought we'd keep him at home, but it was driving him crazy that other kids were going when he couldn't. We were afraid the loneliness would kill him even quicker."

"How long?" Sam managed to ask, swallowing down the huge lump that threatened to choke him.

"Tomorrow. Maybe the next day. But he wants to see you. We didn't want to bother you, but ... "

Sam couldn't bear to see the tears that suddenly flooded Mr. Hamilton's eyes, so he looked back at Shane, whose own eyes were now open and fixed on him.

"It's all about perfect practice," Shane whispered when Sam sat next to him. "Maybe you really will be good enough someday."

Tim Anderson read through Sam's curriculum guide, taking notes as he went along. When he reached the end he flipped through the pages again and commented, "You don't teach music at all?"

"They have enough to learn without adding music to the load, Tim. They'll get that next year, with the music teacher."

Tim thought that odd, but didn't feel he should press any further, especially when Sam suddenly got up and left the teachers' lounge, door banging behind him.

"We have enough to live on for a year or so," Sam told his wife, after the kids were in bed and the house was quiet. "I can't do it anymore. I have to quit."

Sam's wife had heard him voice a quiet desire to do something else before, but this was the first time she heard fear when he said it.

"Be sure," was all she could say to him.

"Unless I have a good reason not to, I'll hand in my resignation at the end of the semester."

Normally, when seeing his student teachers bombarded by a dozen big red rubber balls, Sam would have laughed. At the very least he would have grinned.

He couldn't make himself care that much that Tim Anderson was on the wrong end of the dodge ball line. If Tim wound up with a split lip from a well-placed throw, he would react, of course, but he wasn't sure he would really care.

He stood by the classroom door, leaning against the brick wall with his arms crossed in front of himself, and watched the game, trying to ignore the ear-splitting laughter.

Tim Anderson could handle them.

In fact, he decided, Tim would be a good replacement for him. Still young and full of fresh ideas, he would do just fine.

Sam watched the game with a surge of renewed interest, mentally running through a list of things he needed to be sure to tell his successor. He watched so intently that he didn't see the woman who walked up to him, nor the small child whose fingers she gripped with one hand, nor the package she held tightly in the other.

Sam only realized she was there when the small boy sniffed hard. Surprised, Sam pushed off the wall.

"That kind of concentration and devotion is why Shane liked you so much," she said, releasing the boy's hand so she could extend hers to Sam.

"Well, hello," was all he could muster as he shook her hand. The boy was looking up at him expectantly, so Sam offered his hand to him and asked, "And what is your name?"

"Rider," he replied firmly. "I'm four and a half."

Mrs. Hamilton laughed and said, "Rider is just his nickname. But he is four and a half, and looking forward to being in your class next year."

Sam didn't think it was the right time to mention that he didn't intend to be there next year.

"You knew my big brother," Rider stated, impressed by that little bit of trivia.

"Yes, I did. And I liked him very much."

Mrs. Hamilton pulled away the paper from the package she'd been holding tightly. "One of the last things Shane asked us," she said as she ripped away the last shred of paper, "was that we make sure you got this. He wanted you to have it."

Without thinking, Sam reached for it. "But his father gave this to him."

"We have dozens of videotapes of Shane playing it. This is what he wanted, Mr. Moore."

"Yeah," Rider added, "so you hafta have it!"

Sam wrapped his hand around the neck of the guitar, feeling the strings bite into his palm.

There were dozens of things he wanted to say to he, but all he could do was whisper, "Thank you."

"I know five chords," Sam told his students, who were sitting on the floor in front of them. "I learned them just last year—someone your age taught them to me."

He fumbled with the guitar, strumming awkwardly at first, until he felt comfortable with his fingers on the strings.

"I'll play, but you have to sing. *Row Your Boat*, okay?"

Tim was sure the racket could be heard down the hall and into the office, and he couldn't believe that something so unbelievably bad could sound so good. Sam sang as well as he played the guitar. He played for only fifteen minutes, until his fingers hurt and the kids were laughing too hard to sing along. He refused to smile. Because he hated it. Really.

K.A. Thompson is writer living in Northern California with a Spouse Thingy and two psychotic cats. Formerly the editor of *Martial Artists Wired*, she spends much of her time playing online and getting very little accomplished (aside from writing five novels of her own, and helping Max the Psychokitty pen three books.) She is not completely insane, and has that pesky twitching under control now. Visit her blog, Thumper Thinks Out Loud, at http://kathompson.blogspot.com.